LOCKED AWAY

DI SARA RAMSEY #13

M A COMLEY

D1534026

ACKNOWLEDGMENTS

Thank you as always to my rock, my mother, Jean, I'd be lost without you in my life.

Special thanks as always go to @studioenp for their superb cover design expertise.

My heartfelt thanks go to my wonderful editor Abby, my proofreaders Joseph and Jacqueline for spotting all the lingering nits.

Thank you also to my amazing ARC group who help to keep me sane during this process.

To Mary, gone, but never forgotten. I hope you found the peace you were searching for my dear friend.

ALSO BY M A COMLEY

Unfair Justice (a 10,000 word short story)

Irrational Justice (a 10,000 word short story)

Seeking Justice (a 15,000 word novella)

Caring For Justice (a 24,000 word novella)

Savage Justice (a 17,000 word novella Featuring THE UNICORN)

Flawed Justice (a 17,000 word novella)

Gone In Seconds (Justice Again series #1)

Ultimate Dilemma (Justice Again series #2)

Shot of Silence (Justice Again #3)

Taste of Fury (Justice Again #4)

Clever Deception (co-written by Linda S Prather)

Tragic Deception (co-written by Linda S Prather)

Sinful Deception (co-written by Linda S Prather)

Forever Watching You (DI Miranda Carr thriller)

Wrong Place (DI Sally Parker thriller #1)

No Hiding Place (DI Sally Parker thriller #2)

Cold Case (DI Sally Parker thriller#3)

Deadly Encounter (DI Sally Parker thriller #4)

Lost Innocence (DI Sally Parker thriller #5)

Goodbye, My Precious Child (DI Sally Parker #6)

Web of Deceit (DI Sally Parker Novella with Tara Lyons)

The Missing Children (DI Kayli Bright #1)

Killer On The Run (DI Kayli Bright #2)

Hidden Agenda (DI Kayli Bright #3)

Murderous Betrayal (Kayli Bright #4)

Dying Breath (Kayli Bright #5)

Taken (Kayli Bright #6 coming March 2020)

The Hostage Takers (DI Kayli Bright Novella)

No Right to Kill (DI Sara Ramsey #1)

Killer Blow (DI Sara Ramsey #2)

The Dead Can't Speak (DI Sara Ramsey #3)

Deluded (DI Sara Ramsey #4)

The Murder Pact (DI Sara Ramsey #5)

Twisted Revenge (DI Sara Ramsey #6)

The Lies She Told (DI Sara Ramsey #7)

For The Love Of... (DI Sara Ramsey #8)

Run For Your Life (DI Sara Ramsey #9)

Cold Mercy (DI Sara Ramsey #10)

Sign of Evil (DI Sara Ramsey #11)

Indefensible (DI Sara Ramsey #12)

Locked Away (DI Sara Ramsey #13 coming August 2021)

I Know The Truth (A psychological thriller)

She's Gone (A psychological thriller - coming September 2021)

The Caller (co-written with Tara Lyons)

Evil In Disguise – a novel based on True events

Deadly Act (Hero series novella)

Torn Apart (Hero series #1)

End Result (Hero series #2)

In Plain Sight (Hero Series #3)

Double Jeopardy (Hero Series #4)

Criminal Actions (Hero Series #5)

Regrets Mean Nothing (Hero #6)

Prowlers (Hero #7)

Sole Intention (Intention series #1)

Grave Intention (Intention series #2)

Devious Intention (Intention #3)

Merry Widow (A Lorne Simpkins short story)

It's A Dog's Life (A Lorne Simpkins short story)

Carmel Cove Cozy Mystery Series

Murder at the Wedding

Murder at the Hotel

Murder by the Sea

Wellington Cozy Mystery Series

Death on the Coast

Death by Association

A Time To Heal (A Sweet Romance)

A Time For Change (A Sweet Romance)

High Spirits

The Temptation series (Romantic Suspense/New Adult Novellas)

Past Temptation

Lost Temptation

PROLOGUE

*M*onths of preparation, and all would begin to come to fruition today. She turned sideways to study her svelte figure, the one she'd worked hard to achieve over the past year or so. It had definitely been a struggle. At the beginning, the weight she'd been comfortably carrying for years, nearly all her life, had refused to shift until she'd joined the local slimming club. There, the instructor had re-educated her about what food to eat to obtain the best nutrition. The weight had dropped off, once she was taught the secret to good food choices and selecting the healthy options rather than the bad ones. She'd managed to lose six stone in seven months and had claimed the Slimmer of the Week award on numerous occasions, which had given her the extra boost to continue, to thrive to obtain the results she was seeking.

And now, here she was, her first mission complete, which had allowed her to pluck up enough courage to carry out her second task. A dangerous endeavour which would affect a lot of peoples' lives. Hopefully the result would be worth it.

She glanced at the time on her gold-plated watch: ten minutes to spare. Libby tucked her T-shirt into her skinny jeans and threw a cardigan around her shoulders. The weather so far in August had been changeable at best, so it wasn't worth her taking the risk. *Better to be prepared*, echoed her mother's wise words in a corner of her brain. Tears misted her eyes, and she swiped them away, determined not to be distracted. She was a woman on a mission.

After collecting her car keys from the bowl on the console table in the hallway, Libby jumped into her white Golf and headed for the rendezvous.

Libby had persuaded the woman she was getting together with to meet up after her normal working hours. Jennifer had tried to dissuade her, but Libby had developed skills in the art of persuasion over the years. She drew up outside the house, five minutes before the time she was expected. Libby scanned the area, searching for a suitable place to hide until her acquaintance arrived. She'd been following her for weeks and was aware how impeccable her time-keeping was.

She left the car parked outside the building and hid down the alley at the side, tucked away. There was only one route into the road, therefore she knew Jennifer wouldn't spot her as she drove in. Impatience gnawed at her, and she tapped her foot, until the faint sound of a vehicle approaching sparked her interest. Her heart rate almost doubled in the space of a few seconds.

Jennifer drew up and parked behind Libby's Golf. Libby shifted nervously in her position. Sweat greasing her palms, she wiped her hands down her jeans. Jennifer left her car and went to the boot. She removed her work holdall, filled with the tools of her trade, and approached the front door.

Libby waited. Watched the woman's anxiety build as she stood on the doorstep of the old, decrepit building. Then she made her move. Casually walking out of the alley, she strode towards Jennifer who turned to face her, a wide smile stretching her plum-coloured Botoxed lips apart. "Oh, hi, I thought I'd come to the wrong place for a minute there. Jilly, right?"

"That's right. Thanks for coming. It's great to see you again."

Jennifer frowned, and her smile slipped a little. "Sorry, have we met before? I'm usually quite good with names and faces. Can't say I can recall either of yours, though."

"Oh yes, many moons ago."

Jennifer shuffled her feet, looking awkward under Libby's piercing gaze. That was, until Libby broke into a smile and advanced towards the front door.

"Never mind, I'll fill you in later, when I see fit to reveal all," she added mysteriously.

"Okay. If you don't mind me saying, this house seems a little run-down, are you sure the electricity is on?"

"Oh yes, everything is in perfect working order. Never judge a book by its cover, as my dear old mum used to spout, more times than I care to remember."

"Ah, okay. Yes, my gran used to say the same thing, God rest her soul."

"Died recently, did she?"

"A few years back. I miss her terribly. I was close to her, closer than her other grandchildren anyway."

"That's a shame. What did she die of?"

"Old age, damn dementia got her in the end." Jennifer's head dropped, seemingly upset by the tragic circumstances in which her grandmother had passed.

Libby paused for a moment, reassessing what was about to happen, until her inner voice prodded her into action once more. "Such a shame when that happens. More and more dementia around these days. Scary thought. I blame all the processed food people tend to consume. All those E numbers can't be good for you. Why tamper with the natural goodness in food? I stopped eating junk food last year and feel a hundred times better now."

Jennifer's gaze ran the length of Libby's frame. "I must say, you look good on it. You can share some secrets with me while I cut your hair. Mind if we get on with it? I'd like to get home before nine, if possible. I've been at it since eight-thirty this morning. It's been a pig of a day, and I rarely make appointments past six in the evening."

"In that case, I appreciate you fitting me in. Yes, let's crack on, shall we?"

Jennifer picked up her holdall. Before she could straighten up,

Libby withdrew the length of metal from the back of her jeans and whacked her over the head. Jennifer tumbled to the ground.

Great! How the heck am I supposed to get her in the car now?

Brute force turned out to be the answer. Luckily, Libby had combined her weight loss with getting fit at the gym, lifting weights heavier than she'd ever dreamed she'd be able to manage to lift. Her instructor, Dwayne, had pushed her to her limits with the mantra of 'No pain, no gain' ringing in her ears.

Jennifer was lighter than she first appeared. Once her stance was correct, Libby had no problem lifting her dead weight and placing Jennifer in the boot of her car. She wasn't bothered about leaving her victim's car at the scene, there was no way it could come back and bite her in the arse in the future. She'd been far too careful in her plans to slip up at the first hurdle. She drove to the designated place where she had prepared to hold Jennifer and the others. All she needed to do now was keep them fed and watered for a few days. Easy, right?

Her willingness to abduct the women quickly and hold them together would be an extreme challenge for her, she realised that. But this scheme had taken months of planning. She kept her fingers crossed that all would go swimmingly over the days to come. Her mission would be complete by the end of the week at the latest, and then the real fun would begin.

She placed the limp Jennifer in her temporary cell, out cold on her makeshift bed, and retreated from the room, locking the door behind her. Libby peered through the peephole she'd drilled into each door and observed her captive. Still no movement from her. It remained that way for another half an hour, until suddenly, Jennifer stirred. Raising her head slightly off the low bed, she anxiously took a look around her. Libby fought hard to suppress the giggle tickling the back of her throat.

Jennifer's fear was unmistakeable. Tears trickled onto her pale cheeks. Finally, she had the courage to sit up and take a better look at her surroundings. Libby observed her confused expression and smiled. It was how she'd planned it would be. Each of the women would sit in the cell in a confused state until she had them all gathered together. The day of reckoning was just around the corner, for each of them.

1

*S*ara snuggled up to Mark for another five minutes. She hated Monday mornings at the best of times, but this morning would be different, she knew that, and was trying to avoid getting ready for work for as long as possible. DCI Price had insisted she give her an answer to the continuing predicament that had blighted her for the past month or so, by this morning at the very latest.

The outcome would mean she would have no alternative but to sack someone on her team. *Why me? What gives headquarters the right to expect such skulduggery and underhandedness from me? If that's what we could call this. I'm messing with a person's life. I could be putting them under unnecessary stress both emotionally and financially. Is that what my job has come to? Effectively playing God with my team's lives?*

She clung tighter to Mark. He reciprocated, kissed the top of her head and whispered, "It'll be all right in the end, you know that, don't you?"

Sara angled her head and looked up at the man who had saved her from her dark thoughts over two years earlier. "I doubt it. None of this makes sense, Mark. The statistics are there for everyone to see. Crime rates are escalating rapidly now that people are getting back to normal after the pandemic, not that it prevented some twisted buggers giving us the runaround during lockdown. They're paper-pushing idiots. Why would they insist on cutting our man hours?"

"Budgets, we all have them. It must be a bugger to deal with for a large organisation like yours. You know, the police force. At the end of the day, maybe they're just the same as every other business on the go, trying to recoup the inflated costs that our society suffered during twenty-twenty."

"Did your business suffer?" Sara asked the question but already knew what his answer was going to be.

"Slightly, but not to that extent. We kept going, you know we did. But what with people not having the funds in place to care for their pets, I think a lot of animals suffered unnecessarily during the pandemic. Hopefully, most of them haven't suffered irreparable harm, although, I suspect in some cases, the opposite is true. I know we tend to brush all talk about the pandemic under the carpet nowadays, but in reality, there were always going to be consequences to it, not just for a few people but for everyone."

Sara sighed and hugged him. "You're right, as always. In the grand scheme of things, where so many people lost their lives, someone losing their job must seem insignificant to most people, those who still have a regular income to rely on, that is."

"That's true. Have you made up your mind who the person is going to be yet?"

"Honest answer? No. It's been tearing me inside out. It's now crunch time. That wonderful job lies ahead of me today, this morning, first thing to be precise. Before the chief has a chance to jump up and down on my head, demanding answers to a problem she tasked me with solving nearly a month ago. Surely, she should realise how difficult I've found it, leaving the problem unresolved until the last minute."

"Deep down, I bet she's feeling the same as you, love. If not worse. She's the one caught in the middle, after all."

Sara nodded. "Wise words again. I haven't blamed her for putting me in this position. It's a part of the job I've never had to deal with before, and I hope it doesn't land in my lap again in the future, either."

"You're stronger than you think. I have every faith in you doing the right thing, sweetheart. Maybe, once you air the problem with your team, just maybe, one of them will volunteer to take the fall."

"You reckon? Why would anyone give up a career they love?"

"Personal circumstances possibly. Again, going back to the consequences of the pandemic, maybe someone is carrying an extra burden they haven't told you about."

She sat up, covering her naked breasts with the quilt, and stared at him. "Like what?"

"I don't know. Maybe one of them now has to care for a relative with long Covid, I think the term is. Someone suffering from the damage the disease has caused. Has anyone mentioned anything?"

"No, no one, not to my knowledge." She searched her mind, reflecting on what had gone on in the past few months, for any hints some of her team might have dropped, and shook her head. "Nope, nothing is coming to mind. I'd better get up and start my day. Thank you for listening and trying to help solve the issue."

He pulled her in close for a kiss. "You're welcome to use me as a sounding board any day, you know that."

"What would I do without you in my life?"

"You'd cope. You're more resilient than you give yourself credit for."

Her mouth dropped open for a moment. "No way. I'd be lost in this unforgiving wilderness called life, if you weren't by my side for the ride."

"I doubt that's true. Shoo... you're going to be late. Or is that your aim for the day?"

She chuckled. "Damn, you've seen through me yet again. I love you, Mark, don't ever forget how much you've changed my life since we first met."

"Hey, right backatcha. If Misty hadn't been poisoned, I'd still be a lonely bachelor vet eating takeaways every night and sharing my bed with dozens of bed mites instead of a beautiful woman."

She wrinkled her nose at the thought. "Eww... thanks for sharing that ghastly image."

"Sorry. Go. I'll make some breakfast while you're in the shower."

"I knew I married you for a reason."

She darted out of the bed before he could take a swipe at her backside. She took a longer, hotter shower than usual, while she contemplated what lay ahead of her. *Maybe a new crime will have landed on my desk and help me to prolong the decision further. Nah, the chief would come down on me like a ton of bricks if that happened, again. Today is the day, whether I like it or not.*

After going through her usual morning routine, she dressed in a navy-blue suit and descended the stairs, the inviting smell of cooked bacon drawing her to the kitchen. There, sitting on the table, steam wafting from the plate, was a cooked breakfast, consisting of scrambled eggs, bacon, sausage, baked beans and a slice of toast. "Crikey, I swear you're trying to make me fat."

"Nonsense. You're as skinny as the day I first met you, in spite of my efforts to get you to put on an extra few pounds."

She turned sideways and stuck out her stomach, not that there was much to stick out. "Now I know you're telling porkies."

"Sit, stop trying to push your stomach out of shape."

"I won't need to after eating this lot." She took a final glance at the clock. It was eight-fifteen, no need to rush breakfast, it would only take her twenty minutes to drive into work.

Mark sat opposite her with a slightly bigger breakfast. They ate in silence, apart from the odd moan of satisfaction that seeped out now and again. Sara washed her breakfast down with two cups of coffee, kissed her wonderful husband goodbye and left the house.

She pulled up outside the station with ten minutes to spare. She groaned when she saw DCI Carol Price waiting beside her car as Sara parked next to her. Smile pinned in place, she exited the vehicle. "Morning, ma'am, lovely day. I just hope it's not going to be too hot today."

Carol raised an eyebrow. "Why do we Brits always resort to

discussing the weather when something is playing on our minds or we're trying our best to avoid a certain subject?"

"I wasn't aware that I was," Sara replied, her smile never wavering.

"You think you know me, Sara Ramsey, the trouble is, you don't. I, on the other hand, can read you like a damn book. Don't try and pull a fast one on me again." She leaned in and lowered her voice. "Have you made your decision yet?"

"Kind of."

"What? You're cutting it close to the wire. You have until midday to give me your answer, or did that particular fact slip your mind?"

"No, I'm fully aware of the time restraint you have laid at my door, thanks, boss."

Carol narrowed her eyes. "Bollocks, it's not me and you know it. We're in this together, Sara, you'd be wise to remember that."

"I know. I hope we don't fall out about this. I've sensed a little tension in the air since this issue was first discussed."

"Nothing on my part, I can assure you. We all have responsibilities we need to overcome and deal with as necessary. Some are more pleasant than others. It sucks that I've had to force your hand with this one, I didn't mean to, but you kept dodging the bullet, so to speak, and did your best to avoid dealing with the issue head-on."

"So, I'm to blame for headquarter's failings now, is that it?"

"Don't talk shit, Sara. No one is to blame. It's to do with making the job viable for all of us." She opened up the main entrance door and held it open for Sara to follow her into the building.

"If you insist," Sara bit back, her mood darkening since she'd arrived in the car park.

The chief stared at her and shook her head. Without saying a word, Price stomped up the stairs ahead of her. Sara gulped, annoyed that she had vented her anger on her superior, not for the first time over the last few weeks.

"Sorry," she called after her boss.

Her apology was ignored. She stopped off at the ladies' toilets to check her appearance in the mirror and to give herself a pep talk at the same time. "Get a grip. Stop snapping at people and get a frigging grip, for everyone's sake."

The toilet flushed in the locked cubicle behind her, and she cringed as the door opened and Carla emerged.

"Talking to yourself again? Should I be concerned about you?"

"Good morning. No, not yet." She held her arms out to the sides and slapped them against her thighs. "Today is the day." She took a moment to check the other cubicles were not in use. "I'm a wreck already. Just had a run-in with the chief in the car park, which has pissed me off."

"You're putting too much pressure on yourself, Sara. Give yourself a break. This isn't down to you. Yes, you're the one who has been instructed to fire the bullet but you're quite within your rights to pass the buck on this one. Blame headquarters, it's their fault after all, not yours. You hear me?"

Sara appreciated Carla's insightful words, but it would never put a different spin on things. "I hear you. The countdown has begun anyway, I'm going to announce it to the team this morning. They can discuss it between themselves until eleven-forty-five. After that, I need a definitive name to present to the chief so that she can issue the chop and give the unlucky person all the details. I genuinely hate my job at times. I've never, ever had to deal with something as major as this in my life before, not professionally," she added, after her first husband's murder back in Liverpool fleetingly shot through her mind.

"You haven't had it easy over the years and, believe me when I say this, I wouldn't want to be in your shoes right now. I'm glad you confided in me, I feel it has eased the burden on your shoulders slightly."

"It did. Just not enough to prevent the guilt surfacing once more. Okay, deep breath, I guess I'm ready for the shit to hit the fan now. Stand well back when it does, act surprised, as though this is the first you've heard about the issue, okay?"

"Right, if that's what you want. Would you like me to grill you? Kick off a little? How do you want me to react to the news?"

"It would be better if most of the verbal assault came from you, I suppose."

Carla winked at her. "I promise not to hold back."

Sara slapped a hand to her face and shook her head. "Shit! What have I let myself in for now?"

Carla then did something Sara hadn't been expecting. She hugged her and patted her on the shoulder. "You'll be fine. Have confidence that the outcome will be for the best."

"If you say so. Let's go and see what lies in store for us as we enter the lions' den."

Carla chuckled. "Slight exaggeration there. You're the boss, you have orders just like the rest of us. The team will understand and appreciate that, I promise you."

"They're the best team around, that's why I'm so hesitant to tear them apart."

"Have faith. Something might rear its head that will make the chore a little easier to swallow, for all concerned."

"I hope so."

They left the ladies', and Carla pushed the door to the incident room open ahead of her. "Coffee?"

"Silly question." The team were all at their desks. "Morning all. As we don't have an open case at the moment, now is the right time to run something past you that I've been dealing with for the last month or so. Carla will be handing out the drinks; put your orders in and then gather around, if you will? Christine, maybe you can lend her a hand, distributing the cups?"

"On it, boss." Christine left her seat and joined Carla.

Before long, the two women had bought and dispensed the coffees.

Sara pulled a chair out from the nearest available desk and sat down. She crossed and uncrossed her legs a number of times until she found a comfortable position to begin. "Okay, what I'm about to say will come as a huge shock to most of you, if not all of you."

"Are you leaving us?" Carla demanded.

Sara shook her head. "That would be wishful thinking on your part, I believe, DS Jameson."

"That's a tad unfair," Carla bit back, folding her arms.

"Sorry. This is a hard enough undertaking as it is, please don't make it any harder than it needs to be."

"I'll try not to. Sounds ominous. Let's have it, boss," Carla replied, the look in her eyes telling Sara everything was going to be all right.

Sara smiled and let out a long sigh to prepare herself. "I was instructed by the DCI, who was only following instructions from head-quaters, to cull a member of staff. Sorry, that's laying things on the line, rather than sugar-coating it, I owe you that much."

"What?" Carla shouted. "Cull? As in give one of us the boot? How come? We're such a successful team, why would they even consider breaking us up?"

"Believe me, I've been battling this stupidity for a full month now. Today we have reached the ultimate deadline, where I have to provide a name for the chop, for want of a better word. Does anyone have any thoughts?"

"For what? Giving up our pension at the drop of a hat?" Carla shouted back. "They've got to be bloody joking, pulling your leg, boss. They have to be. Why on earth would they even consider breaking up an experienced team like ours?"

"It's the cuts, Carla. I promise you, I've done all I could. Every waking minute of the day we haven't been chasing criminals, I've been proactive, trying my very best to fight for everyone's job. At one point I even spoke about handing in my own notice, if it would help. I was chastised for being childish. Not how I'd anticipated that conversation going, I can assure you. So, what do we think, guys?"

The team all looked at each other and shrugged. Everyone kept their mouths shut. An awkward silence descended until Christine raised her hand to speak.

"Go on, Christine. What's your take on this scenario?"

"I suppose, if push came to shove, boss, I could hand my notice in. Scott and I have been talking about having a baby recently, anyway."

"Really?" Sara asked, her mood lightening with the prospect of a successful outcome until it dawned on her she'd be losing one of the team's greatest assets. Christine was their shit-hot computer expert.

"But wait, that won't do. You're far too experienced to consider being without. You have excellent skills we mere mortals are lacking."

"Oh, yes, I hadn't really thought about that, boss."

Sara smiled at the constable and scanned the other faces staring at her. Each of them wore a pained expression, which chipped away at her heart. "Anyone else?" she asked timidly.

Again, the silence jarred with her. Until Sara glanced in Will's direction. He was fidgeting in his seat and fiddling with his tie. Will was forty-six now, a detective sergeant with over twenty years on the force. *Hmm... close to retirement age. Closer than anyone else on the team, I suppose.* She took a gamble. "Will, do you have anything to say on the subject?"

"As it happens, plenty, ma'am."

Sara cringed, hating the word. "Care to share with us?"

"Well, I suppose my age would count against me, if you were to carefully scrutinise each and every one of us. Why don't I make it easy for you?"

Sara uncrossed her legs and sat forward, her elbows digging into her thighs for a moment until she relaxed her position. "What are you saying, Will?"

"I'm saying I would be willing to hand in my resignation, if it came to the crunch. Let's face it, I'm an outsider really, compared to the rest of you."

Sara shook her head. "You're no such thing, Will. You're just as valuable to this team as the rest of us are."

"Whatever." He shrugged, and his gaze fell to the floor.

"Are you serious about resigning?" Sara prompted, her pulse racing. She hadn't expected the dreaded undertaking to be as easy as this, never in a million years.

Will stretched his legs out in front of him and placed his hands behind his head. "The more I think about it, the more the idea is growing on me. Hey, I'd like to make one thing clear, though, if I may?"

"Go ahead."

"I'm going to miss you guys if I do go. Anyway, it would stop the missus nagging me about not being able to take off at a moment's notice to go on a bargain holiday when they crop up. And there's the added bonus of having a lie-in, of course."

The team all laughed, and Craig threw a screwed-up piece of paper at his colleague. "Idiot, you'll be missed, Will. I agree with the boss, you are a valued member of the team. Although, one thing I won't miss is the dreadful jokes you bombard us with daily. I'm sure your wife will appreciate hearing them all day long."

"Shit! Never thought about that. I bet she'll end up on a murder charge before long, being forced to put up with me twenty-four-seven."

The team all laughed, even Sara cracked her face as the relief flooded through her that a solution had been found at last. Had she seriously considered each of the team members and their different attributes, she supposed she would have come to the same conclusion Will had come to in the end. "Are you sure, Will? Wouldn't you rather discuss the situation with your wife first before you hand in your notice?"

"Not really. It's about time I grew a pair and made a decision of my own without her sticking her oar in. Nope, I'm definite about my decision, ma'am. When do you want me to leave?"

"Crikey, I haven't thought that far ahead. Let me have a word with the chief and get back to you. Bugger, I'm stunned by how quickly this issue has been resolved, given the length of time I've been fretting about it."

"I've felt a tad stale for a while, if I'm honest," Will replied.

"You should have spoken up," Sara said. She rose from her seat, itching to get on the phone to the chief to break the news she was anticipating.

"You know me, I plod on regardless."

"Well, we're going to miss your smiling face around here, Will."

He snorted. "Now I know you're fibbing."

Sara approached him, stuck out her hand, and he slipped his into hers. "It's true. You're as much a part of this team as anyone else, and I've never had any reason to doubt your abilities during any cases we've worked on together." She turned to face the rest of them. "That goes for everyone. Which is why I've been going through hell for the past few weeks, since the chief first raised the issue with me."

Will smiled. "Your problem, ma'am, is that you're too sensitive. You had a job to do, you should have asked the question and left it up to us to decide. As Christine stated, everyone likely has something going on in their lives that could have been considered."

"You're right. I appreciate you guys more than you'll ever know." A large lump appeared in her throat, and before the others could see the tears pricking her eyes, she coughed slightly and rushed into her office. There, she sat behind her desk. Trying to compose herself for the next five minutes, she tinkered with the post vying for her attention until she felt ready to place the call the chief was expecting.

Finally, she felt calm enough to ring the chief.

"Yes."

"Sorry to disturb you, ma'am. I thought you'd want to hear the news right away."

"Well, don't leave me hanging, DI Ramsey. What news are you referring to?"

Sara inhaled a large breath and let it out as she spoke. "The news that has been a thorn in the side for both of us over the past month. Someone has volunteered to resign from their post."

"Oh, I see. And who might that person be? And don't tell me it's you."

Sara laughed. "I've already tried that one and got nowhere. No, it's Will Rogerson I find myself indebted to."

"Will Rogerson," the chief replied quietly, as if mulling over who that could be. "Ah, yes, I recall him now. That's good news then, he's not far off retirement, so won't be much out of pocket, you must be relieved by the decision, Sara."

"Not really, ma'am, it amounts to the same thing, more stress on the rest of us, what with being a man down."

"I know it'll take some getting used to, but you and your team will do it. I'm confident about that. You're a competent bunch."

"Okay, now the *who* is out of the way, I suppose the next step would be to obtain the *when* from you. How long will I have his services for before he leaves?"

"He'll need to work another month, so make sure you get your money's worth out of him."

"That's a terrible thing to say, ma'am."

Carol Price laughed. "Sorry, my wicked sense of humour coming to the fore there. Will you send Will my regards and thanks for stepping up to the plate?"

"I'll do that. I'll try to organise a farewell party for him as well, near the end."

"Good. I'll even chip in twenty quid, how's that?"

"Generous to a fault as usual, ma'am."

Carol chuckled. "On that sarcastic note, I'll let you get on with your day, Inspector. Good luck."

"Thanks." Sara ended the call and returned to give Will the news that he would be working with them for another four weeks.

"Great news, thanks, boss. That'll give me a couple of weeks to search for the right words to tell the missus. Now that the revelation has had time to sink in, I have to say I'm not looking forward to telling Mrs Rogerson. Maybe I should search for another job ASAP, it'll soften the blow."

Sara smiled. She'd been fortunate to meet Will's wife on the odd occasion and she'd found the woman to be very aloof during the meetings, as if she was only attending to appease her husband. "Take all the time you need searching for a job, Will. If you have to attend any interviews, let me know, I'll grant you the time off, no problem, okay?"

"That's very kind of you. I'll do that, boss."

Carla came to stand next to her, notebook in hand.

"What's up? A new case?"

"Possibly. I've had a report of a young woman going missing. Something sparked my interest. I know we only occasionally work missing person cases, but I wondered if we should take a look into this one."

Sara shrugged. "It's not as if anything else has landed on our desks, is it? Yep, let's go for it. Get the details ready, I'll down my lukewarm cup of coffee while I take a peep through the post and be with you in a jiffy."

"Okay." Carla returned to her desk while Sara went back to her office.

Sara cast a cursory glance through the post, opening what grabbed her attention the most. She found nothing new within the envelopes so she relegated them to her in-tray and returned to the incident room. "Right, Carla, do you want to fill me in en route?"

"Sounds good to me."

"See you later, folks. Keep tidying up any loose paperwork lying around from the previous case, until we get back. Oh, and Will, the chief sends her gratitude."

"No problem, boss."

Sara squeezed his shoulder as she passed. "It's appreciated more than you realise."

She caught up with her partner in the hallway. Carla said, "That was a relief, wasn't it?"

"I should say. I never expected it, did you?"

"Nope, not at all. He's right about one thing," Carla added.

"What's that?"

They descended the concrete stairs together.

Carla leaned over and said quietly, "Out of all of them, he didn't really fit in."

Sara hitched up a shoulder. "I can't say I've noticed over the years. He's always chipped in when it was needed. Maybe upon reflection, he did seem to hold back a little compared to the rest of the team. Either way, we're going to be a man down by the beginning of September, which is only going to heap more pressure on the rest of our shoulders."

"Bring it on." Carla smiled, punching the air.

Sara glanced her way and burst out laughing. "I'll remind you of that little outburst when we're drowning in paperwork and pulling our hair out over the next few months."

"Ever wish you could take something back?"

"Frequently."

They breezed through the reception area and got into the car.

Sara turned the key in the ignition, and Carla set up the satnav. "We're heading out towards Munstone, do you know it?" Carla asked.

"Nope, can't say I've come across that one before. I'll wait for the dreaded automated voice to issue her command and then head in that direction."

"I'm getting there. Give me two secs."

"How are things at home?" Sara asked, filling in the time.

"You might be able to multitask, but not everyone is as capable as you."

"Sorry. I thought you could." Sara drummed her fingers on the steering wheel until she saw Carla shake her head.

"There you go. I think we're good now."

Sara set off, followed the voice's instructions to turn left out of the gate and then tried again. "So, how are things between you and Gary?" She was chuffed with herself, successfully managing to say his name without flinching, for a change.

"All is fine at home. What about you and Mark?"

"We're hunky-dory as always. He's an absolute treasure. Cooked me breakfast again this morning before I left the house."

"Bloody hell, you've got him well trained."

Sara sniggered. "Hardly, he wants to do nice things for me. Doesn't Gary ever bend over backwards to make you feel special?"

"Nope, next question."

Sara shot her partner a quick look. "That's a shame. Are you sure you're a good match, Carla?"

"Do you mind paying attention to the road? You're making me nervous."

Sara's gaze drifted back to the road ahead. "Sorry. You haven't answered my question."

"Is it obligatory? You know we usually end up having a tiff every time my love life is discussed."

"Do we? Can't say I've noticed that. I care about you, love, sorry if that's wrong of me."

"It's not." Carla sighed. "Sara, not everyone has a lovey-dovey relationship like you do. You're lucky to have found a man like Mark, who treats you as an equal. Most women aren't that fortunate."

"Are you referring to yourself there?"

"Maybe. I haven't decided just yet. Gary is still dealing with getting used to his injuries after the accident. I guess we need to take tentative steps, see what each day brings us."

"That's been months, though, love. He should have recovered well enough by now. What's his physio said, anything?"

"It's going to take time and that we both need to be patient."

"That must be frustrating for both of you to handle."

Carla let out a heavy sigh. "It's worse for him. My feelings don't count, not really."

Sara gasped. "Of course they do. You have a God-given right to a life of your own. You're still young, don't waste it, Carla."

"Waste what, my life? I'm with the man I love, how can that be deemed as wasting my life?" Carla snapped.

Sara squirmed in her seat. It hadn't been her intention to start a row with her partner; all she was trying to do was to give Carla her support, if that's what she needed. Gary had treated her appallingly over the past year or so since his accident. They had broken up once but got back together after they had both been abducted by someone Gary owed money to. That incident, against Sara's better judgement, had brought them closer together. Something Sara could foresee causing problems in the future. She decided to let Carla's question hang in the air between them and concentrate on the satnav instructions instead.

They passed the Premier Inn, and Sara took a right at the roundabout. "What's the name of the missing person? You'd better fill me in before we get there."

Carla flicked open her notebook. "Jennifer Moore, she's a mobile hairdresser. Her husband reported her missing yesterday—actually, Saturday night—but he was told to leave it twenty-four hours and to call back if she hadn't returned in that time. She hadn't, so he rang the station last night."

"Why are we only just hearing about this now?"

"My fault. I rang the reception desk, keen to know if there were any new crimes that could be of interest to us, and bingo, Jeff thought this one might be a good match, considering the couple of missing person cases we've successfully solved in the last eighteen months. I know it's not our preferred crime to deal with, but I thought I'd take a punt anyway."

"I hear you. It's better to be busy rather than sitting on our hands back at the station, although, saying that, I'm sure I could find some much-needed paperwork I could wade through at a push."

"Yeah, but would that be enough fun to fill your day?"

Sara took her eyes off the road for a second, faced Carla and smiled. "Hardly. What's the husband's name?"

"Alex Moore."

"Okay, here we are now. Let's see what the rub is."

They exited the vehicle. Sara pressed the key fob to lock the doors and approached the quaint cottage tucked back off the road behind a large privet hedge. Once they had found the path leading up to the front door, Sara gasped at the stunning garden, a rainbow of colours before them. "Bloody hell, look at this. How old are these people?"

"What's that got to do with anything?"

"You don't expect youngsters to have the time to look after a garden as well as this. Even Mum and Dad's garden is poor by comparison, and they're out there all the time."

"Doh, maybe they have a gardener come in a few times a week to tend to it."

Sara clicked her fingers. "Good shout. I never thought of that. Thanks for pointing out the obvious, I think my brain is still recovering from the weekend barbecue we had."

"Why wasn't I invited?"

"Oh, umm… well…"

Carla laughed. "I was joking. You have your own life to lead outside work hours, boss."

"Actually, we went to our neighbours' house. We take it in turns to host either a dinner party or a barbecue."

"That's so cool. Glad you guys get along so well. Back to work, eh?"

Sara waved a hand, still awestruck by the glorious view of the garden from the gate. "Sorry. You're right."

They wound their way up the snaking path to an oak door with a large ring as a knocker at head height. Sara knocked and searched for her ID in her jacket pocket.

The door was opened within a few seconds by a man in his thirties. His brow furrowed with concern. "Hello. Are you the police?"

Sara and Carla both flashed their warrant cards, and Sara asked, "Yes, sir. Is it Mr Moore?"

"That's right. Come inside. I need to sit down. My legs are all shaky standing here."

"No problem."

They followed him through the cottage. He needed to duck to get through the doorframe to the lounge. A huge inglenook fireplace greeted them.

"Have you been here long, Mr Moore?"

"Around four years, I suppose. Jennifer had driven past this place with a keen eye for a while. As soon as the 'For Sale' board went up, she was on the phone to the agent straight away."

"It's beautiful. Out of interest, how do you manage to keep on top of the garden? It's absolutely stunning."

"Thank you. We inherited its excellent condition and employ the gardener who created it. Neither Jennifer nor I know the first thing about gardening, that was the one drawback I could see buying this place. Anyway, that's not why you've come to see me. Take a seat. Can I get you a drink or something?" He motioned towards the crystal glass half-filled with amber liquid, sitting on the table next to a cosy easy chair. "I needed something strong to calm my nerves. They've been in tatters since Saturday night."

Sara and Carla sat on the sofa close to the unlit fire. "We'll decline, thanks. Sorry it's taken so long for us to get back to you. In instances such as this our hands are tied until the first twenty-four hours have passed."

"Yeah, I get that. It doesn't help the family deal with the stress any better knowing that the police refuse to help. Sorry, I'm angry, I didn't mean to take it out on you. I appreciate you're only doing your job to the best of your ability."

"We have to follow the limitations put in place. To be fair, most people who are reported missing generally show up after a few hours."

"I get that. But this was different. My wife's life could be in danger. She agreed to meet someone, and I haven't heard from her since. Surely that's different to someone just going missing because they wanted to have a break from their family troubles or something along those lines, isn't it?"

"Yes, sir. Okay, you have our full attention. We're going to do our very best to find your wife and bring her home. Perhaps you can tell us what you know about this meeting she attended?"

"She received a call from a woman in desperate need to have her hair done for some sort of award ceremony. Jen doesn't usually take on new clients, but she broke her own rules for this woman because she sounded so desperate. She told Jen that her normal hairdresser had let her down at the last minute and that she would double her fee if she could fit her in. We're in the process of saving for an exotic holiday to the Maldives, therefore Jen jumped at the chance to help the woman out."

"I see. And can you tell us where she was due to meet?"

His head dipped. "No, I switched off, the live match was on and... I feel really bad about not taking notice of what she was telling me, especially in the circumstances. You can imagine what horrors have been going through my mind every time I think of Jen showing up there and not reporting back to me. Sorry, that sounded bad, I mean checking in with me. My mind is a mess."

"I can imagine. Can you give me your wife's phone number? We'll try and trace the call."

He reeled off the number, and Carla jotted the information down in her notebook.

"What about the client's name, did you get that?"

"Yes, Jilly Smallcombe," he said, without hesitation.

"Ah, that's a start, at least. We'll check through the records available to us and try to locate the woman ASAP. Maybe you can give me an idea of what type of character your wife is?"

He scratched the side of his neck and heaved out a sigh. "She's what you would call temperamental, I suppose. Most of the time she's easy-going, but there are certain things that push her buttons, and when that happens, she erupts like Mount Vesuvius."

"Care to enlighten us about what those triggers are?" Sara asked, intrigued.

"Any type of sports, she hates them. Also, when I tend to come home drunk from the pub via a taxi. I suppose she thinks the money would be better spent on a holiday rather than lining a landlord's and a taxi driver's pockets."

"Anything else?"

"She detests people who are stupid, you know, who ask daft questions."

"In what respect?"

"Any respect. She's quite well-educated, she trained to be a solicitor but she's always said it was her calling to be a hairdresser. Yeah, I know, hard to figure that one out, isn't it? A vast difference in salaries, that's for sure. I put up with it because it keeps her happy."

"And she's a mobile hairdresser, is that right?"

"Yes, she has an extensive client list. Booked up for months, she is. People rarely let her down for fear they won't get another slot for weeks. She's good at her job, very professional. Has all the right gear to ply her trade."

"And her vehicle? Does she travel by car or does she have some kind of professional van at her disposal?"

"No, just a basic car. It's nothing special, a Ford estate. She's thought about getting a van but would rather visit people's homes instead of turning up expecting her clients to climb in the back of a van. This time of year, they can be stuffy as hell and in the winter as cold as an igloo, that's what discouraged her from buying one in the end. Plus, it would have cost a fortune to set up. That's the whole idea of being a mobile hairdresser, to keep the costs low."

"I can understand that. And your wife hasn't had any other dealings with this Jilly Smallcombe in the past?"

"No, none at all. Christ, why did she take the bloody job on in the first place? It's not like we need the money, not really, and she went against her work ethics, too."

"Meaning what?"

"Not fitting someone in off the cuff like that. She's fastidious about keeping her appointments structured. She allows herself half an hour for lunch every day and rarely works evenings."

"So why did she change her mind this time? Because of the money?"

"Yes, it proved too tempting to resist and…"

"And?" Sara prompted, easing forward in her seat.

"And I guess I ticked her off by saying I'd invited a few of the guys around to watch a match on TV. She was far from impressed."

"Ah, that makes sense. I take it you've rung her mobile?"

He looked at Sara and raised an eyebrow. "You think I'm stupid or something?"

"No, it was a simple question."

"I did. It didn't connect. Not sure what that means, maybe her battery ran out or something. I'm as confused about that, along with everything else that's happened. My wife is missing, and I believe something bad has happened to her. There, I've said it out loud. I hope for her sake that I'm way off the mark with that theory. Please, are you going to help me, help her, or not?"

"Of course we are. I'm sorry if we've given you the impression we're not interested, nothing could be further from the truth. It's our job to investigate every angle of the missing person's life. The more you can tell us about her character and her working life the easier it's going to be for us to find her."

"I get that."

"Good. Now, this is probably an angle you won't want to divulge. I'm going to ask you some deeply personal questions. It will be in your wife's best interest if you tell us the truth and don't hold back."

"Meaning what?" His eyes bored into hers.

"Can you tell me if you have a happy marriage? Any problems in the past we should know about?"

"No. Definitely not. I love my wife. Yes, she can get shirty with me now and again when I do something to tick her off, but that's part and parcel of being married, isn't it?"

"I suppose. When was the last time you fell out with each other?"

"What? You want me to conjure up a specific date, is that what you're getting at?"

"Just roughly… are we talking about a few weeks, months or years?"

He paused to think for a couple of moments. "Hmm… let me think. Yes, that was it, it was on her birthday, back in May. I had arranged a secret party, invited a few of her friends off Facebook, but when she rolled up thirty minutes later, she was livid that I'd arranged things behind her back and even more furious that she wasn't dressed for the occasion. There had been a fierce downpour, and she'd got drenched and truly wasn't looking her best, in her eyes." He shook his head and continued, "She looked as beautiful as ever to me. But she was having none of it, stormed upstairs and stayed in her room all night. Some of her friends went up to see if she was all right, but she refused point blank to speak to them. So, I sent everyone packing and dumped all the food I'd bought in the bin. She didn't speak to me for the rest of the week. Eventually, she calmed down enough to forgive me. Which was a relief."

"May I ask why?"

"Because the way she was ranting and raving, damn, I thought we were heading for the divorce courts, that's why!"

"And she hasn't fallen out with anyone else recently?"

"No. To be fair, she's been uber-busy, six days a week."

"She's totally committed to her work, is that what you're telling me?"

"Yes and no. To the work fifty percent but also saving for this damn holiday. Her motto is, work hard and play harder. Except not in this country, not with the foul weather we usually get."

Sara smiled, understanding his wife's point of view completely, although she much preferred to take her chances in this country, exploring what the UK had to offer.

"Can you give us a recent photo of your wife, sir?"

He stood and searched for his phone in his jeans pocket, scrolled through it and handed it to Sara. On it was the picture of a beautiful blonde woman with sparkling, bright-green eyes.

"That's perfect. Would you mind sending it to my phone?" She gave him the number, and within seconds her phone pinged, informing her she'd been sent a text message. Sara checked the image had arrived with the text and nodded. "Excellent. We can get the photo circulated as soon as we get back to the station."

The doorbell rang. Alex excused himself and rushed out of the room to answer it. Voices mumbled in the hallway for a few moments, then the door opened to reveal an older man and woman standing behind Alex.

"These are Jennifer's parents, Josie and Les Warren. They've come to see if there has been any progress. I told them you've not long arrived."

Sara stood and shook the newcomers' hands. "Pleased to meet you both. I'm DI Sara Ramsey, and this is my partner, DS Carla Jameson."

Josie stared at Sara's hand before shaking it. "What are you doing about our daughter's disappearance? We've all been out of our minds with worry since Saturday. I may be speaking out of turn—if I am, please don't hold it against us—but I think it's appalling it's taken you so long to get here."

"I'm sorry you feel that way. We're issued with strict guidelines we need to follow. It's frowned upon by those at headquaters if we don't adhere to them."

Josie tutted and shook her head. "Sick, that's what it is, when someone's life could be in danger."

Smile still intact, Sara said, "I couldn't agree more. We're here now. I want to assure you all that you've got the best team in the area handling your daughter's case. If she's out there, we'll find her."

"*If she's out there?*" Mr Warren challenged, his brow furrowed either in anger or frustration, Sara couldn't tell which.

Sara refused to be cornered by him. Instead, she nodded and told them all, "Right, if there's nothing further anyone wishes to add, we should be on our way."

"I've got plenty I want to add," Mrs Warren blustered.

Sara noticed the weary expression exchange between Alex and his father-in-law. She prepared herself for another barrage of insults.

Mrs Warren sucked in a large breath and crumpled before their eyes. Sara was the first to react. She led the woman to the sofa and eased her onto it.

"I'm sorry. The thought of someone abducting my only child is... I haven't slept since I heard the news. My mind is playing havoc, going over different scenarios. I can't stop the strange and dangerous thoughts from rattling around in my head. I want my daughter back. Please, please, bring her home to us."

Sara smiled and stroked the woman's arm. "Obviously, I can't make any promises but I can give you my assurance that we'll do our very best to bring your daughter back to you. I know the delay hasn't been acceptable to you, but take my word for it, it's still very early days and you need to retain the hope in your heart."

"I'm trying, I swear I am. Have there been any other cases such as this?"

"Nothing that has come to our attention in the last week or so."

"Why? Why lead my daughter into a trap and kidnap her? What reason would anyone have to do that?"

Sara smiled and sighed. "That's what we need to find out if that's what even happened. When was the last time you spoke to Jennifer?"

"Friday evening."

"How did she seem to you?"

"The same as usual. Although I did detect a note of weariness in her voice. I pleaded with her to take the weekend off, but she refused. She's an utter professional. Told me she had no intention of letting her clients down just because she needed some time off. She'd have her break in a few weeks when she could afford to book a last-minute holi-day. If only she hadn't accepted that last appointment."

"I know. We're going to do our very best to track down the person she was due to meet. We must be prepared that the person might be innocent and that something could have possibly happened to her en route to the rendezvous, though, again, it's something we're going to need to look into."

"I don't think that thought has occurred to either of us, has it, Les?"

"In truth, I don't know what to think. No, wait, here's my thought on it: I don't think we should hold the officers up, they have a job to do, out there; they won't find Jennifer sitting around here, will they?"

"Hush now, Les, don't be so bloody rude," Mrs Warren chastised her husband and then cradled Sara's hand in her own. "Ignore him, he's always been an impatient bugger from the day I kept him waiting half an hour at the church on our wedding day."

Her husband grunted and threw himself into the easy chair beside him.

"Actually, your husband is correct. If there's nothing else you can tell us, it would be better if we made a move. Set the investigation rolling." She released her hand from the woman's and stood.

Carla followed her to the door.

"Here's my card." Sara offered it to Alex. "Ring me if you think of anything else we haven't covered here today."

"I'll show you out."

"Goodbye, Mr and Mrs Warren."

"Goodbye, do your best for us," Mrs Warren shouted.

"We will," Sara called over her shoulder.

Alex rolled his eyes as he wished them good luck at the front door. "At least you get to leave. I'm bound to have them here for a good few hours yet."

"I'm sorry. I'm sure their hearts are in the right place," Sara assured him.

"I know. Do what you can to bring Jen home to me, I'm begging you."

"I promise. I'll be in touch soon, hopefully."

Sara and Carla left the quaint cottage and hopped back in the car. Carla let out a long breath.

"And breathe," she muttered. "I thought we'd have to listen to her banging on for an hour or more. I was willing you to take the plunge and leave."

"Glad I didn't disappoint you then, partner. Give her some slack, put yourself in her shoes. Hey, come to that, I think I reacted in the same way when you were bloody abducted last month. Despite your experience with criminals, I still feared for your life. Imagine what they must be going through."

"That's shot me down in flames. Thanks for that."

Sara punched her partner in the thigh. "Don't go getting all mardy on me."

"I'm not. And if it's all the same to you, I've been doing my best not to dwell on my abduction. Therefore, I'd appreciate it if you didn't keep referring to it all the time."

"All the time? Hardly, but your wish is my command. I'm sorry it's still raw for you. Have you thought about extra counselling sessions? They might help in this instance."

"No. I'd rather just forget about it and move on. I know having to deal with cases such as this is going to make that difficult at times, but if I have to go into battle every time a kidnapping case comes our way if that's what this is, then that's what I'll have to do. Trust me, it's harder than you realise."

Sara twisted in her seat. "You know I'm here for you night and day, don't you?"

A smile twitched at Carla's lips. "I do. But I'm trying my very best to deal with the issue by myself and not get anyone else involved."

"What about Gary? He's supportive of your needs, isn't he?"

Carla leaned back against the headrest. "Don't start, Sara. Leave him out of this, okay?"

"Whoa! What? I only asked a simple question, and you snap my head off for it."

"I didn't, but that's beside the point. I know how you feel about Gary. Every time his name is mentioned, don't think I don't notice your reaction."

"All right, I admit it. I care what happens to you, love. Pardon me for looking out for a friend."

Carla sighed, lowered her head and stared at the road. "Can we concentrate on the case instead of my troubled love life?"

"So you admit there's something wrong with your relationship?"

"Leave it, Sara, it was a slip of the tongue, one I'd rather not elucidate on. Where to now?"

"If you insist. I repeat, I'm always here for you, no matter what. Back to the station." Sara started the car and drove back into town.

Carla didn't say another word on the trip. Sara sighed a few times, fearing that she'd overstepped the mark with her partner, not for the first time regarding her relationship with her waste-of-space boyfriend, whom she perceived played on his injuries to keep Carla onside.

*B*ack at the station, Sara brought the rest of the team up to date with the information they had gathered about the missing person. "Therefore, we need to try and find this Jilly Smallcombe, the mystery client she was supposed to have met on Saturday evening. Use every conceivable database available to us. I want Jennifer found ASAP."

"What about her car, boss?" Craig asked.

"I'll leave that in your capable hands, Craig. If we can locate that it might give us some clue as to what happened to Jennifer. There again, it might not."

"On it now." Craig grinned.

Sara chuckled inside, his enthusiasm top notch as usual.

She left them to it. After an hour of Sara trawling through her dreaded post, she returned to catch up with the team. "Right, I know I'm expecting you all to have worked miracles in my absence, but let's have it."

A sea of blank faces glanced her way.

Christine was the first to offer anything. "I've checked the electoral roll for a Jilly Smallcombe, and our database just in case she had a record of sorts, and nothing. It's as if she doesn't exist."

Sara perched her backside on the desk nearest to her, folded one arm and placed the forefinger of her right hand to the side of her face.

"That's news I wasn't expecting to hear. So where does that leave us? Craig, what about the car?"

He shook his head. "I've issued an alert on the vehicle. We could be waiting days to hear back, boss."

"Not good. So, if her name doesn't exist, what does that tell us? That she intentionally led Jennifer into a trap? It seems plausible to me, but why? And more to the point, what the hell has she done with Jennifer? Could she be holding her somewhere?"

Carla let out an exasperated sigh. "If she's still alive. What if she was intentionally set up by this woman so that she could kill Jennifer?"

"Again, it's something we need to consider. Until we find something worth latching on to, we're stumped. Craig, keep on top of the car situation, I think that's going to be pivotal. Also, can you see if the ANPR system picked up Jennifer's car at any time on Saturday evening?"

"I'll see what I can find. I might need someone to lend me a hand, boss."

"You've got it. Will, can you oblige?"

Will left his chair and pulled up the nearest one next to Craig, and they put their heads down.

Sara stared long and hard at the details on the whiteboard, trying to figure out what they were missing. "Premeditated, that's my assumption, but why? According to Alex, her husband, Jennifer is a character who, well, she's hard to describe really. I suppose *professional* would be out there in front, although he did say she wasn't an easy person to live with. That doesn't give someone the right to kidnap her, though, but think about things logically, it might spark something. Could she have irritated someone to the extent that they might want to punish her for it? There again, I could be talking out of my arse. Probably the latter, but what else do we have to go on at this stage? Nothing."

"The investigation has only just started, it's a bit harsh to say we don't have anything right now," Carla suggested.

"I know, but it also happens to be the truth." Frustration was already kicking Sara's backside on this one. "Why would someone kidnap a hairdresser? It's not like she can be used to obtain valuable information. They're not rich, at least they don't appear to be."

"Umm... wait, didn't Alex say she trained to be a solicitor?"

Sara nodded. "That's right. Carla, do some digging into that side of things for me. Good shout. It seems the more likely possibility to me."

The more she mulled over the idea, the more Sara thought her partner was right.

2

*L*ibby paced the corridor, every so often peering through the spyhole in the cell housing Jennifer. Her usually hard exterior crumbling before Libby's eyes. Jennifer likely heard her footsteps approach the door, but Libby tortured her further by ignoring Jennifer's pleas for help.

She'd recently fed her prisoner a bowl of porridge, more than she deserved. But Jennifer had refused the food. Now the bowl lay on the floor before her, the porridge a stodgy clump at her feet.

"Please, please, why are you doing this? Who are you? Do I know you? What have I ever done to you to deserve to be treated like an animal? To be caged up like this? Show yourself, let's discuss the rights and wrongs of this situation. I know you don't want to hurt me, not really, otherwise you would have done it by now. Please, let me go. I promise I won't tell anyone you've kept me here. My poor husband will be beside himself with worry. Don't let him suffer. I love him. He needs me. He's not capable of looking after himself, he never has been. Please, let me go home and care for him, like a wife should."

Libby closed her eyes to block out Jennifer's incessant moaning, pleading and pathetic questions. But her eyes flew open when she heard the final sentence of Jennifer's plea. *How dare she use that as an excuse to let her go? How fucking dare she go down that route? She wouldn't have a clue what it was like… she might think she knows, but she knows fuck all about the sacrifices concerned. You're going to suffer for saying that, missus. You're a pathetic human being, a selfish individual who prefers to hear the sound of her own voice rather than listen to other people's pleas for help. A wicked, no, evil bitch who revels in destroying people's lives. Who used to take pleasure in punishing those perceived weaker than herself. Well, I've got news for you, bitch, this biatch is no longer weak and unable to defend herself. You'll find out soon enough what I have planned for you and the others, but first I need to gather the rest of them.*

She glanced at her watch. It was nearly ten-thirty, time to make a move. She knew her second target would be finishing her shift soon, and the pub where she worked was on the other side of town, giving Libby barely enough time to get there.

Libby took one final look through the cell door at Jennifer, banged on the door to get her attention and whispered, "Fear not, little one, you'll have company very soon."

"Who's there? Please, you have to let me go. What do you mean by that? Who are you?"

Libby tipped back her head and laughed her way up the wide corridor. She secured the door to the storage unit behind her and jumped into her car. She drove fast but ensured she kept below the speed limit, to avoid being picked up by any police cars in town as she passed through the city centre and out the other side. She pulled up outside the pub with five minutes to spare, at eleven-twenty-five, aware that Smith would exit at eleven-thirty on the dot, as usual. Libby parked next to the barmaid's vehicle in the corner of the car park. She switched off her lights and hunkered down in her seat until a rowdy drunk was kicked out of the pub and staggered her way.

Fuck off, you drunken git. Go on, bugger off home to your faithful, obliging wife that you'll probably maul in bed tonight, whilst dribbling and farting. I bet you even fall asleep while you're poking her one, and it won't be the last time either. Yuck, why do women put up with men who down gallons of booze? How can most folk afford to get that drunk, what with the price of beer and spirits nowadays? Go on, fuck off, get out of my sight before Smith comes out. You've got precisely two minutes, arsehole. Now shift your frigging self. Or I'll be forced to take you out. Yes, that's what I'll do, kill him if he doesn't move on quickly.

The drunk straightened up and scanned the area all around him. Libby sensed he was about to do something uncivilised right in front of her damn car. She waited and watched. He fiddled with the zip on his jeans and dropped his trousers. She groaned inwardly. If the bastard didn't complete his shit soon, she was going to miss the opportunity to grab Smith.

Fuck off! Do one, you cruddy individual.

He must have heard her. Somehow, he managed to right himself and pull up his jeans. He let out a large belch and scampered out of the car park, probably feeling ten pounds lighter, judging by what he'd unloaded in front of her car.

Vile bloody creature. I hope your wife gives you hell when you get home. If I was married to you... yeah, the likelihood of that would be zilch, I would have throttled you years ago.

Her eyes were drawn back to the main entrance of the pub, her mind now rid of the interruption, her focus one hundred percent returned to the job in hand.

Her pulse raced. She hated hanging around for people, even if they were only a few minutes late. The door opened, and a man shouted farewell to Amanda Smith. The brunette left the pub and walked in her direction, or should that be *tottered* in her higher-than-average heels?

Jesus, they must be at least five inches. Has she worked all night in those? Or changed into them before she left the pub? Does it frigging matter?

She set the questions aside in her mind and waited until the woman was close enough to attack. Libby's hand was poised on the door handle, and she was ready to burst out of hiding at a moment's notice. Another few feet and she'd walk into the trap Libby had set for her. Amanda came to a stop at the boot of her car, her eye drawn to something lying by the passenger door. She peered over her shoulder to check no one was around before she made her move.

Amanda dashed the final couple of steps and bent to pick up the ten-pound note from the ground. Libby had stuck it down with Blu-Tack to prevent the wind from whisking it away. Libby held her nerve and then struck. Bam! She opened her car door—it connected with force, with Amanda's head. Libby slipped out of the car, dressed all in black for what she had in mind. The woman was slumped on the ground. Libby raced to the boot, opened it and returned to Amanda. It took all her strength to lift the woman, who was a good twenty pounds heavier than Jennifer to shift. She made a mental note to add more weights to her bar when she worked out later.

Libby threw Amanda in the boot, a small groan escaping the woman's mouth as she dropped the lid. Then Libby ran around the car, jumped in the driver's seat and drove out of the car park before anyone else left the pub. She'd been staking out the place for a few weeks, noting Amanda's routine and what happened after she finished work. Libby was aware no one left the pub after the barmaid, at least they hadn't in all the time she'd been on patrol.

She drove back to the lockup sporting a huge grin, pleased with her successful mission to capture yet another one. *Two down, only three more to grab, and then the fun can begin. Maybe I'll up my workload and snatch two of them tomorrow. I'll check my notes when I get home later and see if it's feasible. It would definitely make my life easier if I could collect them quicker.* She mulled the idea over in her mind until she reached the location. *Concentrate on the task in hand. I need to keep my wits about me in case one of them tries anything stupid.*

She opened the boot and stared at the woman curled up in a ball. Cautiously, she prodded her in the back to see if there was any reaction. There was none. She remained vigilant and hoisted the woman's body out of the car. Libby inspected Amanda's face thoroughly, searching for any sign of consciousness. When she found none, she slammed down the door and made her way to the front of the building. Key in hand, she pushed the squeaking door open and kicked it shut behind her once she'd carried Amanda over the threshold.

Libby felt the woman stir in her arms. She upped her pace. Arriving at the entrance to the cells, she opened the door, keeping one eye ahead of her and the other on the stirring woman. *A few more steps and...* Suddenly Amanda lashed out. Libby was unprepared; she dropped the woman. Amanda landed on her feet but staggered, still dazed from the bang she'd received to her head. Her hand touched her temple in confusion.

"What the hell? Who are you? What are you doing to me?"

Libby pounced on Amanda and punched her in the face, hard enough to knock her out again. Her energy sapped, she dragged Amanda to the cell next door to Jennifer's and threw her on the thin mattress. She'd already put a bottle of water in the cell, ready for when she woke. Apart from the buckets, one for washing, the other for peeing in, the cell would be empty.

Amanda stirred once more. "Where...? What...? Who are you? No, you can't do this to me. I won't let you." Amanda tried to get to her feet, but her attempt faltered at the first base, and she slumped back, groaning and holding her hands on either side of her head.

"Succumb to it, Amanda. All will be revealed soon enough, then the games will begin." Libby laughed and left the cell. She closed the door and peered through the peephole to observe her new acquisition. Amanda's movements were juddery at best. Her limbs flaying as she tried to grab hold of something that would help her to sit upright. There was nothing available, Libby wasn't that foolish. She'd thought long and hard about the needs of the women and also what not to put in the cells, mainly anything which could be used as a weapon against her, if the women tried to strike out.

Amanda's frustration showed through her tears. She sobbed and curled into the foetal position on her makeshift bed. Libby laughed and moved to the next cell. She peered in to see Jennifer staring at her from her bed.

"You have a cellmate now. So there's no need for you to feel so lonely." She laughed again and then left the lockup. Libby drove back to her three-bedroom semi. As soon as she arrived, she completed an hour's session in her well-designed gym on the ground floor. By the end of her workout, she was sweating like the proverbial pig and smelt like one, too. She jumped in the shower and made herself a quick cheese and pickle sandwich and then hopped into bed. Instead of falling asleep right away, she contemplated her next move. Switching the light back on, she dug under her pillow for her notebook and flicked through to find the relevant page. The next two victims' names were prominently written at the top of the page. She refreshed her memory with their individual schedules, and a plan soon formulated in her tired mind. A plan that in the end, kept her awake until the early hours. After that, she fell asleep only to wake at four, soaked in sweat due to the nightmare she'd had. The same nightmare she'd suffered for the past eighteen to twenty years; it was hard to pinpoint exactly when they had started. Although she knew the circumstances all too well. She sighed heavily and swiped the stray tears away, annoyed by their existence. In her opinion, tears were a sign of weakness, and she was anything but weak these days. Once upon a time, she had been perceived as weak to some... But no one could label her as such now.

She had a strength she'd worked exceptionally hard to develop. Adapting her life to work out, to gain the strength and power to obtain a clear goal in her life. She was almost there now. Another few days, and all the pieces of the puzzle would be in place. All her ducks in a row and the five women who had ruined her life for years, all sitting behind bars wondering what the fuck was about to happen to them. Then, and only then, would she feel a sense of achievement. And then, the games could begin...

3

*S*ara drove into work with an ominous feeling gnawing at her insides. She hated it when that happened, there was no rhyme or reason for it, not yet, not this early into an investigation. She tried hard to shrug the sensation off during her journey but failed.

Jeff greeted her with a weary smile as she entered the station. "Morning, DI Ramsey, how are you today?"

"I'm okay, Jeff. What's with the long face and the dimmed smile? Something up?"

"You'll see for yourself very soon."

"That's a bit vague, even for you. Come on, let's hear it."

He shook his head. "Nope, I wouldn't want to spoil the surprise."

"Hmm... now you've got me worried. Is it to do with the case we're working at present?"

"Nope. Guess again, although saying that, I wouldn't mind having a word in your shell-like about something that is bugging me."

"Okay, first things first. What surprise is awaiting me upstairs?"

"If I told you that, it wouldn't be a surprise, would it?"

Sara was getting the impression the surprise awaiting her wasn't going to be a welcome one. Setting that aside for the time being, she asked, "What about the case? What's bugging you about it?"

"Well, as you know, I always check through the overnight reports first thing in the morning."

"I do. You're amazing, not everyone thinks to do that. Has something occurred that I should know about?"

"Possibly. I've made a note to run it past you. Let me fish out the report."

Sara tapped her foot while he went off to find the paperwork. He returned a few seconds later and read from the sheet of paper.

"This came in around one this morning from a Roderick Adams. He was reporting his fiancée, Amanda Smith, as a missing person. Beside himself, he is, apparently."

"Hmm… and you think there could be a link to our investigation? Missing people are frequently reported, Jeff, I don't have to remind you about that, do I?"

"No, ma'am. But this feels different. Maybe it's me talking out of my large backside, but you know nine times out of ten this job is about gut reaction."

"I do. All right, if it will make you feel better, we'll look into it."

"I know you have to officially wait twenty-four hours, but I also know when something doesn't feel right."

"I'm on it. Now, going back to this surprise you mentioned."

He shook his head. "Maybe surprise is the wrong word. My lips are sealed. You'll see soon."

"It's sounding more and more unpromising by the second, Jeff. Go on, give me a hint."

The phone rang on his desk. He glanced at it and then back at Sara. "Saved by the bell."

She snatched up the report and punched her number into the security keypad which opened up to the inner sanctum. She suddenly feared what awaited her as her legs reluctantly carried her upstairs. All became clear the instant she pushed open the door to the incident room. The team all had their heads down, working. No one bothered to glance up and say good morning; that in itself was rare and put her on the back foot immediately. She walked a few steps and stopped at Carla's desk. Her partner buried her head deeper into the paperwork she was holding. Sara hooked a finger under Carla's chin, forcing her to look up at her.

Sara gasped, her legs turning into a wobbling mess beneath her at the sight of her partner's colourful face. Black and blue around both eyes, and her nose was split at the top. "Jesus, fucking... right, in my office, lady. Now."

Sara swallowed down the bile burning her throat. *What the fuck am I going to say to her? If I speak out about Gary she's only going to tell me I'm biased towards him. But what the bloody hell... he had no right mistreating her this way. What a fucking animal he is!*

Sara flung open the door to her office. It hit the wall behind and rebounded, catching her on the arm. "Shit!" She glanced behind her to ensure Carla was following. She was. Sara paced the area beside her desk until her partner entered the room. "Sit down."

"Don't start, Sara, or should I call you *boss* when you're about to give me a bollocking?"

"Fuck off, Carla. This is between you and me. Nothing official, not yet."

Carla threw herself into the chair. Her hands covered her face, and her shoulders jigged up and down as the sobs broke free.

Sara wrenched the door open and shouted, "Christine, two coffees, if you will. I'll reimburse you later."

"Coming right up, boss."

She slammed the door shut again. "Don't say a word until I get some caffeine down me. Scratch that. Answer me this, are you okay? Apart from the bloody obvious."

Carla inhaled a shuddering breath. "I think so. Be gentle with me. I couldn't stand it if you wiped the floor with me."

"I won't, I promise. Oh God, I fear I'm about to break my promise to you. I can't sit back and ignore this, love."

The door opened, and Christine entered the room. She placed the cups on the table and squeezed Carla's shoulder on the way out. Once the door was shut behind her, Sara sat in her chair and stared at her partner across the mound of brown envelopes screeching out for her attention.

"Go easy on me, Sara. I don't want to fall out with you over this."

"What's that supposed to mean? You're not telling me you're going to forgive him, again?"

Carla's chin hit her chest, and her hands dropped into her lap. "He's ill."

"Jesus! No way, Carla, don't let him get away with it, not again. If he truly loved you, he'd worship the ground you walked on, not try to beat you to a pulp. Surely you don't need me to tell you that, love. Come on, think about this rationally."

"I am. This is my fault. I provoked him."

"Bollocks. Don't you dare sit there and tell me that. Even if you did, he should have enough willpower in him to not lash out with his fists. Shitting hell, have you seen the state of your face?"

"No. I refused to look at my reflection. Maybe I should have rung in sick today."

"What? And spend the day at home with that lunatic? No, you're better off with us here. Jesus, you need to see a doctor. I'm going to arrange for the duty doc to come and see you."

Carla reached out a hand to try to prevent her making the call, but she winced at the movement. Sara leapt out of her chair and ran around the desk. Before Carla had a chance to realise what was going on, Sara untucked Carla's blouse swiftly and lifted it. There, the bruises matched the ones on Carla's face. "Fucking hell. Look at you! I can't, no, I won't ignore this, Carla, and neither should you."

"It's so hard. You don't understand."

"I understand Gary is nothing but a flagrant bully. An abusive man who needs to be pulled over the coals, sweetheart. Please, don't stick up for him. This has nothing to do with him being ill. Shame on him for blaming his foul mood on his accident and the damage it left him to deal with day in, day out. Jesus, if you let him get away with this… well, it's going to say more about you than him. Do you seriously want people to think of you as being a weak female? Women have been fighting decades for equality in this life, and you're sitting there telling me that you're prepared to take the punishment he persists inflicting on you without objection. If you do that, you're seriously going to go down in my estimation, love."

"If you'll let me get a word in…"

Sara stepped back, perched on the edge of her desk and crossed her arms. "I'm all ears. Make it good, Carla."

Her partner remained silent for a while, her head still in the same defeated position which Sara was thankful for; that way she wouldn't need to hold back the vomit if she was forced to see the damage to Carla's beautiful face.

"Carla? Speak to me," she prompted softly.

"I can't find the words I want to express. I feel numb right now. Numb and, I don't know how else to describe what I'm going through. I'm aware how weak you think I am. I can't prevent you thinking that of me. All I can do is give you my perspective of life living with someone who used to be a hundred percent fit and now is slightly incapacitated."

Sara lifted a hand to prevent her from saying anything else. "Let me point out a word you just used before you continue."

Carla raised her head and tilted it, looking confused. "What's that?"

"*Slightly* incapacitated, not fully, only *slightly*. From what you've told me in the last few months, he's virtually back to full fitness, so please, please don't insult my intelligence by making excuses for this vile abuser."

Carla's eyes closed, and she shook her head. "Don't call him one of those."

"Why not? If you had bothered to look at your reflection this morning, you would have seen for yourself what a bloody mess your face is in."

"But he loves me."

Sara tipped her head back and growled. "He loves to *beat* you. Why can't you see that for yourself?"

Silence.

"Carla, talk to me."

"I can't because we view things differently. I love him, I can see the good side in him that others fail to see."

Sara covered her eyes with one hand, then let it slip down her face until it was resting on her chin. "I don't know what to say to make you see sense."

"Don't try."

"I should send you home but I'm afraid to. Afraid to put you back there in the firing line. Tell me this, has he shown any form of remorse?"

"No," she replied without hesitation.

Sara flung an arm in the air, got to her feet and marched around her desk. "Bloody hell. I don't know what more I can say to you. Apart from this: if ever a man laid his fist on me, he wouldn't be frigging alive to brag about his triumphs, he'd be rotting in an unmarked grave, probably buried at sea, where the fish could feed off his miserable body."

"That's where we differ, obviously. I see his lashing out as a cry for help."

Sara groaned. "Seriously? And when we've dealt with women who have been knocked around by their fellas, are you telling me you've always felt sorry for the abuser?"

"No. That's different. They're strangers. Everyone's relationship is different. Mine happens to be complex."

"Complex? Jesus, in that case, the sooner you get professional help for your wayward thoughts the better."

"That's a bit harsh, even for you, Sara."

"In my opinion, it's the truth. No matter what I say, you're still going to stick up for him. I'm wasting my breath, I can tell I am. I've never said this to anyone before, Carla, but, my girl, you need to wake up. Look ahead, see where this could end up. I fear for you. You need to put your foot down now and end this abuse before…"

"Go on, don't stop there."

"Before you either end up in hospital or worse still, in a bloody mortuary. Because believe me, one day he'll attack you and not know when to stop."

"He won't. I won't let it go that far."

Sara stared at her partner and shook her head. "You really believe you'll be able to prevent him going all the way, don't you?"

"Yes."

"Did you manage to stop him last night or did he run out of steam after he'd vented his fucking anger?"

Carla's head dropping again gave her the answer she was seeking.

"Right, I've heard enough. I refuse to sit back and not do anything. I'm going to haul his fucking arse in here and have it out with him."

Carla shot out of her chair, placed her hands on the desk and leaned in. "No. I won't allow you to. I resign. I've had it with you." She stormed out of the room before what she'd said had a chance to register with Sara.

Had it with me? What the fuck did I do wrong, except say I thought Gary should be punished for assaulting her?

Dazed, she got to her feet and flew out of the office. She searched the room for Carla; she was nowhere to be seen. "Where is she?"

Christine rolled her eyes. "She grabbed her bag and bolted, boss. When I asked her what was wrong, she grumbled something about resigning, burst into tears and ran out before anyone could ask her what she meant or even stop her. What's going on, boss?"

Sara flopped into the nearby chair, placed her elbows on her thighs and put a hand on either side of her head. "It all got out of hand. I told her she needed to lay charges on Gary, or words to that effect." Her head muzzy, the clarity of the conversation was lost on her. "No, what I actually said was that I was going to haul his arse in here and have it out with him."

"Crikey! Go you. I think I would have said the same if I was in your position. He can't be allowed to get away with this, can he?"

"He shouldn't. However, if Carla allows him to get away with it there's nothing we can do about it. He's scum, I can't stand the bastard. I'm afraid she's noticed that I detest him, and things deteriorated quickly between us. The truth is, I wished I'd kept my mouth shut, but how could I? He needs to be punished for beating her to a pulp. You know what, she hasn't even looked at herself in the mirror this morning. Had she had the courage to do so, maybe we wouldn't be in this position now."

"And what position might that be, may I ask?"

Sara cringed, recognising the voice coming from directly behind her. She gulped and swivelled in her chair to face DCI Price. "Umm... maybe we should discuss this in my office, ma'am."

"Very well, after you, Inspector Ramsey. Be quick about it, I have a meeting with the Superintendent planned in an hour, I'd rather not be late if it's all the same to you."

Sara apprehensively led the way back into her office. She passed by Christine and muttered, "Wish me luck."

"Good luck," Christine whispered back.

Carol Price was already seated, sighing heavily when Sara entered the office. Sara closed the door, inhaled a few deep breaths and took her seat opposite. "I was on my way to come and see you, ma'am."

"It didn't seem that way to me. What position? What's going on? And spare me the minor details, get to the bullet points right from the get-go, will you?"

Sara picked up a pen and jiggled it through her fingers. "The problem is, we're one man down."

"Okay, you've coped with someone being off sick before, what's the trouble this time?"

"Correction, we're a woman down..."

"Either way, it doesn't matter. Get to the point, I'm ordering you, Inspector."

"Carla stormed out."

The chief's brow wrinkled, and her eyes narrowed into tiny slits. "Stormed out? Am I supposed to interpret what that means, apart from the bloody obvious? You're going to need to give me more than that, and quickly, do I have to remind you about the time restraint I'm under?"

Sara sighed. "She turned up for work looking like a poor replacement for Mike Tyson's sparring partner."

"You're not making any sense. Who is Mike Tyson?"

She groaned. "The boxer. What I'm trying to tell you in a ham-fisted way, is that Carla had been assaulted."

"What? Not again. That poor cow. Hang on a sec, if she bothered to turn up for work this morning, why wouldn't she stick around? More to the point, why would she 'storm out' as you put it?" She tapped her watch to emphasise her need for Sara to reveal all swiftly.

"This time it was different. Her fella knocked seven bells out of her. After listening to her constantly making excuses for him, well, I blew my top, told her I was going to bring him in for questioning. I actually used much firmer words than that. Her reaction was to take flight."

"Oh, I see. She'll be back. She just needs to calm down a little first."

Sara shook her head. *Here we go, once I reveal the truth, she's going to go spare!* "That's not all. Her final words to me were that... umm..."

"Spit it out, woman."

"She resigned."

Carol's expression darkened, and her gaze darted towards the window. After a brief pause, she demanded, "She did what? Was she bloody serious? How did it come to this? Why did you hound her?"

"Whoa! I said what every self-respecting woman would say in my situation. Are you telling me you would have listened to her making excuses for that bastard and not reacted?"

"No, I'm not saying that at all, but bloody hell, Sara, telling her you were going to arrest him..." Carol sat back and shook her head.

"What? You can't put this on my shoulders. All I was doing was pointing out to her how wrong she was to accept his illness or his injuries were to blame for him lashing out. You should have frigging seen the state she was in. If you don't believe me how bad she was, I'm sure the rest of the team will back me up. Furthermore, it wasn't just her face that was black and blue. I lifted her shirt, and her ribs had taken a hammering as well. It wouldn't surprise me if she had a couple of broken ribs thrown into the mix, too. And Lord knows what else, she could be bruised all over for all I know. I said what I had to say to a friend and colleague. I had no idea she would bloody react the way she did." She replaced the breath she'd used up and began again. "Any woman with a conscience would have reacted the same way as me. I couldn't sit back and watch her suffer and keep my mouth shut. He deserves to be brought in, put in a cell and be set upon by a dozen officers for what he's put that girl through over this past year or so."

"Why did they get back together?"

"Fucked if I know. Again, I think Carla must have felt sorry for him after they were both abducted. I suppose near-death syndrome would have been a major factor, perhaps."

"Jesus. I can't do anything about this now, my meeting has to take priority. But if you let me have her address, I'll call round and have a word. See if I can't iron things out between you. She's a good person, an exceptional copper, we'd be foolish to stand back and let her walk away. What would she do if she wasn't a copper?"

"I doubt if that thought has even crossed her mind. One thing is for sure, if she gave up her job, it would mean they would be with each other twenty-four-seven, and I can only foresee one outcome to that."

"I trust your instincts. I still think you handled the situation the wrong way, but what's done is done. Do me a favour, jot down her address for me."

Sara reached for a pen and paper, jotted down the requested information and handed it to the chief. "I'm sorry. I realise now that I was in the wrong. I thought I was sticking up for a friend and a colleague. I misjudged the situation. I refuse to keep defending my actions. I think one apology is enough, don't you?"

Carol didn't answer. She rose from her chair and made her way to the door. "We'll see what happens when I pop round and see her later. If she's as bad as you say she is, I'm not sure if I'll be able to bite my tongue either. However, what I do recognise is she needs our support, not our reprimands. We'll see how things pan out."

Sara hung her head in shame. The chief was right, she should have swallowed down the anger she was dealing with and openly listened to Carla's needs. Now it might be too late for that. *I might have lost her as a friend as well as a partner.* She stared out at the white fluffy clouds sweeping past the window for a few moments before she tackled the day's post.

Christine popped her head around the door a second or two later. "Just checking you're all right, boss."

"I'll be fine, full of regrets, but fine nonetheless. Tell Craig to prepare himself, he'll be coming out on the road with me today. I'll be another five minutes here."

"I will, boss."

Christine left her to it. Sara looked down at the first envelope. It had a wet patch on it where a stray tear had fallen. *Daft mare! Get a grip!*

She resisted the temptation to call her husband. To hear his comforting words that everything would be all right.

Ten minutes later, her daily chore dealt with in the quickest time possible, she walked into the incident room to find Craig sitting at his desk, staring at her door. Once she emerged from her office, he bounced to his feet like an overexcited Labrador.

"Okay, I forgot to mention, with all that has gone on here today, that Jeff collared me on the way in this morning, informed me that another possible abduction could be on the agenda. We'll go and see the next of kin now to get an idea of what we're dealing with. I need you guys to continue with what you were doing regarding Jennifer Moore. The young lady we're concerned about is an Amanda Smith— at present, that's all I know about her. I know we're a woman down, but do your best. See you later."

Sara and Craig left the station.

Outside, en route to her car, Craig asked quietly, "Do you think she'll be back?"

"Who? Carla?" Sara replied, looking at him over the top of the car.

"Yes. She seemed pretty upset."

"I know. I'm hoping common sense will prevail. The DCI is planning on going around to see her later. I'm hoping she'll be able to talk some sense into her. Until then, matey, you can class yourself as my new sidekick."

The colour rose in his cheeks, and he smiled warmly at her. "I'm thrilled by the promotion, no matter how long it may last. Thank you for giving me the opportunity, boss."

"Hey, and sucking up to the boss isn't acceptable, got that? Just be yourself, Craig, and we'll get along famously."

"You've got it."

They both dived into the car. Sara set the satnav with the co-ordinates and drove out of the car park.

"All right if I ask another question?"

She half-turned to look at him. "Shoot."

"If the DCI fails to talk Carla around, where does that leave us? Apart from up shit creek, that is."

"I'd rather not think about it. I suppose we could always reinstate Will, if we have to."

Craig cleared his throat.

Sara had a feeling she wasn't going to like what he was about to say next. "Go on, give it to me. What are you thinking?"

"Umm... I think Will may have already found alternative employment."

"You're kidding! Really?"

"If my eavesdropping is up to scratch, yes. I overheard him speaking to a friend of his yesterday afternoon about some kind of mercenary work."

Sara slammed on the brakes; luckily there were no vehicles behind her. "You're not pulling my chain, are you?"

"No. I wouldn't do that, boss. He's got an ex-serviceman mate who is working out in the Middle East. Apparently, he told Will to get in touch if he ever fancied a role in his line of work. I don't think Will was relishing being at home with his wife, truth be told."

"But mercenary work? Who'd have thunk it? It's always the quiet ones you have to watch, eh? Come on, let's have it, what secrets do you possess, Craig? I feel as though I've been shafted today. I guess I don't know you guys as well as I thought I did." She started on the journey again.

"Me? I've got nothing, boss, I assure you. I'm just a boring detective constable, hoping that one day his boss will think enough of his work to put him forward for promotion, when the opportunity arises."

"Hey, don't think your efforts have gone unnoticed, matey. Why do you think I've had a tough month trying to decide who was up for the chop? You're all exceptional to me, and the chief appreciates what a horrible situation she put me in."

He beamed beside her. "That's great to hear. If the opportunity comes up, will you put my name forward, boss?"

"Of course I will. If you're eager to get a promotion, why on earth didn't you come and see me sooner?"

"Umm... I didn't want to appear pushy."

Sara tutted. "You're nuts. You're young, Craig, not stupid. Have the courage of your convictions. If you don't ask you don't get, that's the motto my parents instilled into me from a very young age. I'm passing it on to you."

"Thanks, I appreciate it."

I'm glad some members of my team welcome my wise words, even if others refuse to accept them. Carla, you're a damned idiot, but you're also a dear friend. I hope for your sake, you're going to listen to what the chief has to say. We can't all be wrong. Come back to us soon, girl, before it's too late.

*R*oderick Adams was in his driveway, cleaning his Audi when Sara pulled up outside his home. He dropped the sponge into his bucket and wiped his hand on his jeans, already patchy with soap suds and water. He held out his hand for Sara to shake. "You must be the police. I'm Roderick Adams."

Sara shook his hand and smiled. "I'm DI Sara Ramsey, and this is my partner, DC Craig Watson. Sorry to interrupt, would it be possible for us to chat inside?"

"Yes, I can deal with this later. I was trying to keep my mind occupied. I've done a bunch of DIY chores around the house today, rather than sit around stewing on things. It's the not knowing that's hard to handle."

"I'm sure. Let's hear what you have to say and hopefully we can offer some form of solution for you."

"I doubt it. I know when something is wrong, Inspector. Amanda and I have no secrets from each other. We ring each other at least five or six times a day, we're genuine soulmates. I've never liked the term, not really, but it sums up our relationship accurately enough. Sorry, I'm waffling on. I'm nervous and scared about what's happened to her. Please, come inside. I can finish this off later."

They followed him into the small detached house on one of the new estates close to the racecourse near Bobblestock. He invited them to take a seat in the lounge. It was decorated in a subtle grey, pops of mustard yellow in the cushions and throws, with highlights of the same colours in the curtains hanging at the two windows, one overlooking the drive at the front, the other with a view of the walled garden at the rear.

"Perhaps you can tell us what you know about your fiancée's disappearance, Mr Adams?"

"I can try. Please, call me Rod, that way I won't feel as old as my dad." He smiled, but it soon evaporated.

"Of course. In your own time, Rod."

The three of them took a seat.

Rod remained on the edge of his. "She always rings me before leaving work. That way I can get a sandwich made ready for when she walks in the door. I know, I spoil her. She's worth spoiling, though. She's my life, a one-in-a-million type of girl. I miss her and I'm extremely worried about what might have happened to her."

Sara nodded. "Stick to the facts, if you will?"

"Sorry, of course."

"Where does Amanda work?"

He wrung his hands. "She's a barmaid at the Dog and Duck, a couple of miles away."

Sara glanced at Craig who gave a brief nod to acknowledge he knew the pub.

"And you say she rang you, what time was that?" Sara asked.

"Around eleven-twenty-five. She normally leaves the pub about then. I generally stand at the window, waiting for her to arrive. She never came home. I tried ringing her mobile, and it was dead. I was going frantic. Rang my mum, she told me to contact the police straight away. Please, you have to help me find her. I'll be lost without her. Not only that, we're due to get married in a couple of weeks, and there are dozens of arrangements that need sorting before then. She's in charge of that side of things. If we fall behind on the decision-making, I can see the wedding getting called off."

"I understand the urgency behind you finding her, but please, we're going to need you to remain calm. What type of character is she?"

"Loving, can't do enough for people. She hasn't got a selfish bone in her body."

Sara smiled. "Good to hear. Has anything occurred in her private life which could have backfired or have any bearing on her disappearance?"

He frowned. "Sorry, I don't understand what you mean."

"Has she perhaps fallen out with anyone recently?"

"No, she's not the type. She'd rather walk away from an argument than upset anyone."

Sara nodded and looked sideways to see if Craig was taking notes. He was. "Okay, what about you? Have you got into any trouble lately that might come back and bite you?"

"No, I'm pretty boring. Never been involved in anything dodgy, if that's what you're inferring."

"Okay, so we can discard that as a possibility. Have you checked with the pub?"

"Yes, the landlady, Bella, told me Amanda's car is sitting in the car park. Again, once I heard that news, I contacted the police. I know something dreadful has happened to her. I'm begging you to take this seriously. The woman I spoke to at the police station told me you can't do anything for twenty-four hours; I'm scared that's going to be too late."

Sara smiled again to try to reassure him. "We're prepared to overlook protocol in your fiancée's case."

"You are? That's brilliant news. May I ask why?"

She drew in a deep breath. "Because we're investigating a very similar case which materialised at the weekend."

Rod inched forward in his seat. "Oh, God, and you think there's a connection, is that what you're telling me?"

"Possibly, yes."

He scratched the side of his face and frowned. "I haven't seen anything mentioned on the news. Why not?"

"We have very little to go on at present. If we can link the two investigations then we will run an appeal. Of course, problems can occur if we do that and it turns out to be totally different circumstances behind the women's disappearances."

"I see... I think. You're here, I presume you're taking this seriously. Will you be putting it out on the news now?"

"Possibly. We need to get a little more background information from you first. Are you up for that?"

"Yes, I'll do anything to get her back."

"Is Amanda active on social media? If so, which ones?"

"Crikey, now you're asking. I tend to switch off from all that nonsense. I always think it's more aimed at women than men, or is that a sexist comment?"

Sara smiled. "I wouldn't class it as one, not if you're solely stating your opinion. If I name a few, you can tell me if they sound familiar or not."

He nodded.

"Facebook, Twitter, MeWe, Instagram... TikTok, I think is a new one doing the rounds. What about WhatsApp?"

"Hmm... Facebook is a definite and maybe Instagram—that's the one you upload your photos to, isn't it?"

"Yes, that's right. What about the others?"

"I don't think so. None of them ring a bell with me—I know, I'm hopeless. Technology isn't my strong point. Put a football at my feet and I can dribble for England, but put a computer in front of me and I stare at the screen as if it's from bloody outer space. I'm a plain and simple mechanic, no need for computers as such in my job, although they're creeping into some garages nowadays. Thankfully, my boss is as much of a Luddite as I am and has so far steered clear of them."

"Technology is here to stay, I'm afraid. We'll have a look around the other sites. Do you know if she uses her real name on Facebook?"

"I think her real name. I could do a search on my phone, if you give me thirty minutes, that's how long these things generally take me to figure out."

"It's fine. We'll do it when we get back to the station."

Craig fished his phone out of his pocket, and his fingers flew at warp speed across the screen. He angled the phone at Sara.

She peered at it and compared the photo of Amanda on the screen to the picture on the wall of the couple hugging. "Can I?"

Craig handed her the phone.

She showed it to Rod. "If I'm not mistaken, that would be your fiancée, correct?"

"Yep." He cleared his throat as the emotion welled up. "That's her. God, I never thought I'd miss her as much as I do now. What's that saying? You don't know how lucky you are until something or someone is gone. I feel empty, lost and confused."

"Hey, all is not lost yet. You're going to have to keep positive. If she wants to be found, we'll find her."

"What are you saying? Are you suggesting she's taken off with someone? That doesn't make any sense. For a start, we love each other, and if she did take off, how would she do that if her car is still at the pub?"

"Could someone have picked her up from work, perhaps? Possibly given her a lift home if she's had a drink while at work?"

"No, on both counts. You're forgetting that she rang me as she was leaving the pub. If she was going to hitch a ride with someone, she would have told me, we have no secrets. Another thing for you to consider is that she never drinks during the week. Of course, she makes up for that at the weekend, when she's off-duty."

"Okay, so you like to socialise with people, is that right?"

"Now and again. But mostly, we just like to spend time with each other. She's special and deserves to be treated as such. Anyway, most of our evenings are spent going over the details for the wedding. She's a meticulous planner, a super-organised person. Which is another reason why I placed the call as early as I did. If she says she's going to do something, she does it. As in, come straight home from work at the end of her shift."

"Rightio, is there anything else we should know while we're here?"

He picked at the skin at the base of his thumb and refused to look at Sara. She exchanged a puzzled glance with Craig. He shrugged.

"Rod? What aren't you telling us?" Sara urged.

"We're desperate to keep the news from our wedding guests... Damn, she's pregnant."

Sara's heart seemed to drop into her stomach. "Oh no. How long?"

"We think seven to eight weeks. We're waiting a little longer to get the final analysis from the doc. Amanda has an appointment at the end of next week."

"Is there anything else we should know about before we leave?"

"I don't think so. Please, please do your best to bring them both home to me, unharmed."

Sara could see the emotion written in every pore of his face.

"You have my word." She got to her feet.

Craig flipped his notebook shut and followed her and Rod to the front door. Rod shook their hands and closed the door.

"That was a shocker!" Craig mumbled.

Sara didn't reply until she was closer to the car. "Fair took the wind out of my sails, I can tell you. What if this has something to do with Amanda being pregnant?"

"I'm not so sure. I mean, yes, you might be right. I'm just thinking, he mentioned they've kept it quiet up until now."

"Point taken. Let's see what her boss has to say."

They slipped into the car, and Sara drove to the Dog and Duck. There, they spoke with the landlady, Bella Maddox. Bella was an impressive lady, not only in her build but also in the character she portrayed. Sara took to her right away.

"Call me Bella, everyone does. I was shocked when Rod rang me last night to tell me Amanda hadn't made it home. I was that caught up in locking up for the night and getting some kip that I didn't even notice her car was still outside. No excuse on my part, other than it was delivery day yesterday and the draymen got me out of my bed at sixish."

"Understandable, if you've had a long day to be less observant than you are normally. We're assuming that Amanda was abducted, if Rod hasn't heard from her since and her phone is dead. Can you tell us if there was anyone in here last night acting suspicious?"

Bella contemplated the question for a moment. "No, I've had a good think, and I can honestly say, no. We had a lot of locals in here last night. But no strangers. I can't believe someone would abduct her. Rod must be going out of his mind with worry. Those two are inseparable. Such a sweet relationship. After Amanda cleared the final tray in the glass washer, she always rang him to tell him how long she was likely going to be. I asked her why she followed the same routine after every shift. She told me he always had a drink and a sandwich waiting for her for when she finally got home." Bella snorted. "I can see my fella doing that... not."

Sara smiled. *Mark would do the same for me, especially if I worked long hours.* "So, you didn't see anything out of the ordinary? Someone taking a keen interest in talking to Amanda longer than normal, that sort of thing?"

"No. My punters are all friendly, not a bunch of weirdos. I know what there is to know about each and every one of them, and no one has ever given me cause to think badly of them. You know, with some folks you get the heebie-jeebies. Can't say I've ever had that type of thing, not with my punters. That's why I can't believe what's happened to her."

"What about CCTV? I take it you have cameras inside and out?" Sara confirmed her assumption by scanning the room and spotting several cameras positioned towards the bar.

"Of course. I wouldn't be without them. I installed them a few years ago when there was a spate of pubs getting done over by a gang, not sure if you'd remember that or not."

"It's not ringing any bells. I've only been in the area a couple of years, though."

"Hmm… might have been before your time then. Not that it matters. I'm slipping, I never thought to check the footage. Told you it was a bloody long day yesterday. Rod breaking the news in the early hours of this morning meant I had very little sleep last night. No excuse there, I should have bloody checked. Want to go through it together?"

"That would be fantastic."

"Give me a couple of minutes to set things up. Can I get you a coffee while you wait?"

"Brilliant. White and one for me. Craig?"

"The same for me. Thanks."

Bella had a quick word with the barmaid and then went through the door behind the bar.

The barmaid, in her forties, brought their drinks to them within seconds. "There you go. The boss told me you're in need of a caffeine boost."

"Thanks, you're very kind. Do you have time for a brief chat?"

She looked over her shoulder at a couple of punters sitting at the bar. Two men in their sixties, deep in conversation. "I'll have to keep an eye open, but yes, what do you need to know?"

"Whether Amanda mentioned to you if she had any problems, either personally or professionally."

"Not to me. We rarely cross paths, not really. Bella prefers to cover most of the shifts herself, only have one other member of staff on at the same time, you know, to keep costs down. She's always been the same. Some would call her tight, but not me." The barmaid smirked.

"Fair enough. It's her business, she runs it how she sees fit. There are a lot of pubs going out of business, I suppose she's cautious about that."

"Yeah, I hear you. She's a sweetheart, wipes the floor with most of the male bosses I've had in this trade, I can tell you."

"I can imagine."

Bella appeared in the doorway, and the conversation ceased. "Why do I sense I'm being spoken about?"

The barmaid laughed. "Because you're super sensitive. I was only saying nice things, I promise."

"I should think so. The machine is all set up ready for you." Bella gestured for Sara and Craig to follow her through the bar.

They ended up in a large office that was surprisingly tidy. All the other public houses' offices she'd seen the inside of lately left a lot to be desired. The difference between men and women at play, Sara suspected.

"Why don't you take a seat, Inspector? I can work the controls over your shoulder, if that's okay?"

"Go for it. Craig, get ready to take notes."

"Yes, boss," Craig replied, getting out his notebook and pen.

"Right, you can see here, this is the car park at the side, our main one, if you like. In the corner, you can just make out Amanda's BMW."

Sara blew out a frustrated breath. "Only just. Can you run the disc from the time Amanda left the pub?"

"I can." Bella whizzed through the disc and stopped as a brunette wearing jeans and a T-shirt walked out of the main door. "That's her. Gosh, it's so upsetting to see her leaving without a care in the world, not knowing what lies ahead of her."

"Let's hope we pick something valuable up. Just before she left the pub, I noticed a man exiting the door, looking a tad drunk. Do you know him?"

"Ah yes, that's old Barry, can't remember his surname. He'd received some bad news yesterday about an old friend who had passed away. He hit the bottle to drown his sorrows and to celebrate his friend's life. He was buying drinks for all the punters at one point, until I had a word with him. He hasn't got much money to his name as it is, so to be wasting it on others was just silly, and I told him so."

"How did that go down?" Sara asked.

"Not too well. He called me an interfering old biddy. I bristled at that, I can tell you. Old biddy my eye. Bloody cheek. Good job I like him when he's sober, otherwise he would have woken up this morning having been barred from the pub he frequents most nights."

"So he's harmless. Can we follow his movements on camera?"

"Sure. It can't be him, though. He was in a terrible state. I offered to call a taxi to take him home, but he was having none of it."

"Men can be very stubborn, especially when they've got drink inside them. What's that?" Sara peered at the screen. The image was dark as it took place in the farthest corner of the car park. "Is he on the ground there?"

"Seems to be... oh crap!" Craig muttered.

Sara peered harder and then prompted her partner, "What are you seeing, Craig?"

"You don't want to know."

"Umm... yes, I do. Spit it out." Sara shuffled forward in her seat. Her eyes adjusted a little better to what was playing out on the screen. "Oh bugger, I must be seeing things."

"You're not," Craig insisted.

"Would someone mind telling me what's going on?" Bella demanded.

"It would appear that Barry missed the toilets on the way out and decided to drop his trousers in front of Amanda's car."

"Jesus, that's about the grossest thing I've heard this decade. You wait until I see him, he's going to wish... maybe I shouldn't say any more, just in case I find it difficult to restrain myself."

Sara laughed. "It's nothing a couple of buckets of bleach won't solve."

"You reckon? Crikey, I'm shuddering at the thought of dealing with that mess. I actually saw it on the way in and forgot about it. I cursed an unknown dog for leaving his mark, never dreamed it could be human faeces. Filthy bastard. I'll throttle him when I get my hands on him."

"He was probably too drunk to realise what he was doing." Sara had no idea why she was sticking up for the vile individual, except she was keen to avoid being called out for a possible assault charge in the days ahead.

"He did have a skinful, double what he usually drinks. Maybe I'll make an exception this time. He's still a filthy bastard, though, I have no intention of taking that back."

Sara sniggered. "He is. I think we can all agree with you there."

Bella pressed the button on the machine to see what happened next. Amanda left the pub and walked towards her BMW in the corner. Unfortunately, the camera was too far away to pick up her movements once she reached her vehicle.

"What about other cars parked in the area, can you vouch for them?"

Bella went back and forth on the disc and finally pointed to a light-coloured make and model that none of them could distinguish at the rear, next to Amanda's car. "That one there. Can't say I recall ever seeing it here before, but then again, I might be wrong."

"If you can get a copy made for us, we'll hand it in to the lab on the way back, see if they can come up trumps with anything. As it stands, all we have is that it's a light car. It's not ideal, granted."

"I'll create a copy now. Shame I couldn't make your job any easier. So you think she's been abducted?"

"It would appear to be that way to me, given the evidence we have. She didn't confide in you about any fears or anxieties she may have, did she?"

Bella slotted another disc into the machine and set it recording. "No, can't say she did. What about Rod, couldn't he fill in those details for you? No, wait a second, you're not telling me that you suspect him of some form of foul play, are you?"

"No, I don't believe that for an instant. We need to start somewhere, though."

"It's a mystery, that's what it is. I'd hate to be in your shoes trying to solve the case."

"Two cases," Sara blurted out without thinking. She cringed and then peered over her shoulder at Bella. "That's between you and me. I shouldn't have divulged that fact."

"Goodness me. I had no idea. Are you telling me the women of

Hereford are at risk? That someone is targeting and abducting women in this area?"

"Let's just say we've got two cases of abduction we're dealing with at present. Both incidents have taken place within a few days of each other."

Bella slapped a hand on her face and shook her head. "Oh my! Poor Amanda. What the hell would someone's motive be for taking these women?"

"That's for us to find out, *if* we find the two cases are linked. At this stage of an investigation, it's virtually impossible to tell which direction we're going to take, that's why it's imperative we ask all the right questions and get to know the victims inside and out."

"I get that. As far as I'm concerned, Amanda hasn't said or done anything to anyone which might endanger her life in this way. Let's face it, that's what we're talking about here, aren't we? No one kidnaps another human being unless they mean them some harm, right? Shit, what am I saying?"

"More often than not. However, looking on the bright side, my team have had enough experience in dealing with other cases of this nature, to know that sometimes things work out for the best. So we really need to cling on and not let the hope slip away from us."

"That's great to know. I'll keep my eyes and ears open and report back to you if I hear anything strange being said in the bar, how's that?"

Sara smiled. "You read my mind, I was about to ask you to do the same."

Bella ejected the duplicate disc and handed it to Sara. "Just bring her home, she doesn't deserve to be treated this way."

Sara stood and walked towards the door. "We're going to try. Thanks for all your assistance today."

Bella followed her and Craig back through the bar. "No problem. Have you got a card? If I think of anything else I can call you."

"Thanks, again, you pre-empted me." Sara slid a card across the bar, and she and Craig left.

Outside, they studied the area, and then Sara called SOCO to come and pick up Amanda's vehicle.

"May I ask why?" Craig queried.

"Mainly so I can say I've dotted all the I's on the case, Craig. Let's face it, the abductor might have been hiding by the car; there's a succinct possibility that the perpetrator might have touched the vehicle. It's better to be cautious and get it checked out. Sod the cost, if that's what you're going to say next. That's not my concern, not when two women's lives are at risk. Now, let's get back to the station."

"I see, thanks for the clarification, boss. I hope you don't mind me probing."

"Why should I? It's the only way you're going to learn, Craig."

*T*hey arrived back at the station at around three. Sara's stomach had rumbled a few times on the journey back. She'd stopped off outside the baker's down the road and sent Craig in to pick up whatever sandwiches they had left, to feed the team.

A car drew up alongside her. "Sara, get in." It was the chief.

Sara made a face at Craig. "You go on ahead, leave me the tuna on brown, I shouldn't be too long."

"Good luck, boss. Not sure I care for the chief's tone."

"Bugger, can't say I noticed. See you soon, I hope." Sara pulled on the handle and slipped into the passenger seat of the car.

The chief put her foot down on the accelerator and screeched out of the car park.

"Is everything all right, ma'am?"

"What gives you that idea? You two make me sick. You're going to thrash this out, once and for all."

"Excuse me? I haven't got a clue what you're talking about. Where are you taking me? Should I be worried?"

The chief cast her a scathing look and then concentrated on her driving once more. "Don't be so ridiculous, what do you take me for? We're going to see Carla. You two need to sort this shit out, and quickly."

"What? I don't have time for this, boss. I'm working a double investigation. If she wants to walk out on the job then there's not a lot either you or I can do about it to change her mind."

The chief expelled a long, deep breath. "That's where you're wrong. We need Carla on our team. If you have a problem with her then you need to work things out before we can move forward."

"That's utter codswallop and you know it. I'm her superior, not some constable straight out of training college. She made her position perfectly clear this morning. She'd rather spend time at home with an abuser than stick with a job she knows makes a difference in this world."

"Bollocks. You two are buddies. You need to listen to her cries for help and stop judging her."

Sara's eyes bulged, and she stared at the chief. "What? I've done nothing of the sort. What the fucking hell...? Yes, I swore in front of you, I make no apologies for that. I'm vexed about this situation and the fact that you're coming down heavily on me as if I'm the one in the wrong here."

"Compassion—every officer under me should be riddled with it."

Sara folded her arms and grunted. "I repeat, you're being totally unfair."

The chief's gaze left the road. A horn blasted, and she swiftly faced the road again. "Am I? So what if she has a problem with her fella? She's a good copper, and we need her experience to keep us afloat, especially if we're going to be a man down soon."

Sara felt numb. All this was beyond her. For once in her life, she chose to ignore her superior. If she hadn't, she would have likely ripped into the chief for tearing her apart, which in her opinion was wholly unjustified.

The chief took the hint and, thankfully, didn't push the issue. She drove like a madwoman most of the way to Carla's, and they arrived within ten minutes. Sara's pulse rate matched the chief's speed.

"We're here. You play nicely, you hear me?" The chief snatched her key from the ignition and flew out the driver's door, not bothering to wait for a barbed response from Sara.

She followed the chief up the path to Carla's front door. Her glare bored into the back of the chief's head. *What gives her the right to have a pop at me for doing sod all? Should I have tried harder to dissuade Carla in my office? Even if I'm guilty of not doing that, she left the room, and the station, before I realised what she'd said and done.*

A bruised and bewildered-looking Carla opened the door and invited them inside. They followed her into the lounge. Sara quickly scanned the room—it was a mess. Gym equipment was set up at one end and the chairs were all squashed, clumped together at the other. *She told me they had a designated room for his gym equipment, was she lying?*

"Right, I'm going to sit here and mediate while you two sort things out. I'll give you this warning: I will not, I repeat, I will not be leaving this house until we've come to an agreeable solution. Go on, get on with it."

Sara and Carla both stared at the chief. She sat down heavily on one of the sofas and crossed her arms, letting out a few impatient sighs when both Carla and Sara remained quiet.

Eventually, the uncomfortable atmosphere wore Sara down. "How are you feeling, Carla?"

Carla avoided eye contact with her head low onto her chest. "I'm getting there."

"Good to hear."

"Stop! What the fuck is this?" the chief shouted, outrage reddening her cheeks. "You're talking to each other as if you're perfect strangers. Get a bloody life. You're good friends. As such, you should be making a concerted effort to get along. Stop wasting my sodding time!"

Sara shook her head. In her eyes, the chief was talking out of her arse, and she was getting the impression Price blamed her for what had transpired between her and Carla. Which was totally unjust and incomprehensible.

"I'm sorry," Carla suddenly murmured. She raised her head slightly and looked Sara in the eye for a split second before lowering her head again.

"So am I," Sara admitted. "It shouldn't have come to this."

"Why did it?" Carla asked.

Sara heaved out a sigh. "I guess because we're both pig-headed and set in our ways."

The chief applauded. "Glad you're both seeing sense."

Before she could say anything else, the door burst open and in stormed Gary. They all glanced his way. He stood still, his gaze flicking angrily between the three of them. "Aye up, what's going on here then? Looks like a witches' coven. Thinking up spells to get rid of us men, are you?"

"Only one in particular," Sara muttered.

He heard what she said because he marched over to where Sara was sitting and towered over her. Sara's hand slipped into her jacket pocket where she kept her pepper spray. Carla must have sensed what she was about to do because she left her chair and tried to pull Gary away. He stood firm and glared at her. Sara caught the evil glint in his eye and watched Carla visibly shrivel in front of her.

His hand clenched down by his side, he sneered at Carla. "Did I tell you to move?"

Carla gingerly retreated to her seat. Sara glanced at the chief, whose mouth was hanging open, willing her to intervene. She didn't. If Sara didn't stand up for herself, no one else was about to. She cleared her throat. "You need to calm down, Gary."

It was the worst thing she could have said. He closed what little gap there was between them and prodded Sara in the shoulder. "You reckon? You're in my fucking house, uninvited. Why the fuck should I be happy about that?"

"Gary, please, don't do this," Carla said, her voice trembling.

Gary instantly changed direction and was on Carla within two giant steps. He slapped her so hard her head whipped to the right.

Carla's neck cracked. Sara winced and leapt out of her seat to tackle the bastard. "Get your fucking hands off her. You've hit her once too often."

He turned to face Sara, his broad chest inflating along with his mounting anger. He pushed Sara backwards. She stumbled over the chief's feet and ended up on the floor. Sara refused to stay down. She instantly bounced back up and went into battle with the bully, her hand still in her pocket, stroking the spray bottle.

"I said leave her alone. You touch her again and I'll drag you down the cop shop on a charge of GBH, got that?"

He glared at her up and down as if she was something vile he'd stepped in. "Threats don't wash with me, you can ask Carla about that, can't she, bitch?" He threw over his shoulder in Carla's direction.

You fucking moron. How dare you stand there and speak to us like this? Sara glanced at the gobsmacked chief, still sitting glued to her position, her head swivelling between the three of them. *Fucking hell, you're no use.* "Don't speak to Carla like that. What's your problem, Gary? You never used to be like this. Why the sudden change?" She tried reasoning with him, her objective to ease the tension in the room.

A pronounced vein in his temple twitched. "Don't try to psycho-analyse me. Carla is my girlfriend, that gives me rights to treat her how I want to treat her."

"It doesn't," Carla mumbled.

Again, he shot around and pounced on her, slapping her head the other way.

Carla cried out. "No, Gary. No more, stop it!"

"Stop it!" he mimicked nastily.

Sara had seen enough. Before he had a chance to take in what she was about to do, she aimed the can of pepper spray in his face. He yelled and dropped to the floor.

Sara looked at Carla. "Quick, get your cuffs if you have them handy, mine are in the car."

"They're upstairs." Carla raced out of the room.

Gary wiped his face with the bottom of his T-shirt and stumbled to his feet. He stood in front of Sara, challenging her.

She raised the can again and aimed it. "You want more of the same? Come on, Gary, make my day, come at me."

Carla barged into the room and stood behind Gary. "Give me your hands, it's for your own good, Gary."

"Like fuck I will. Screw you, both of you." He looked down at the chief. "You're a witness to this. Are you going to sit there and let them behave like this?"

The chief stood. "No, I'm right behind them. Come willingly, or Inspector Ramsey will do what's necessary to restrain you."

His head bowed, and Sara thought he was about to surrender, but the opposite was true. He charged at her like an outraged bull battling for his life. He connected with Sara, knocking her off her feet. He ended up straddling her. The can got dislodged in the melee. Sara stared up at the brute glaring down at her. Mixed emotions surged through her. Fear the most dominant one.

The next moment, the chief lashed out with something, and Gary flopped on top of her, smothering Sara and suppressing her ability to breathe.

"Quick, Carla, help me get him off her," Price ordered.

Gary was out cold from the bash he'd received from the heavy statue the chief had managed to get hold of. Price and Carla helped manoeuvre Gary's dead weight, sliding him off Sara, enabling her to get to her feet. Once upright, she placed her hands on her knees, sucking in lungfuls of air, replacing that which had been bashed out of her.

"We need to get the cuffs on him, he could wake up any second."

Carla snapped the cuffs on her boyfriend's wrists, tears trailing down her bruised and swollen face. "I'm such an idiot. I'm so sorry for involving you both in this. You shouldn't have come here today."

"What? Carla, we've seen how he treats you with our own eyes. No woman should have to deal with that shit. You have a right to lead a perfectly normal life, without living in fear of saying the wrong thing and suffering the repercussions for having an opinion of your own. He's in the wrong, *not* you," she pointed out with a pained expression.

"Please, he never used to be like this, it's only since the accident and the abduction."

Sara's mouth gaped open and then she asked, "Wait, does he blame you for being abducted?"

Carla nodded.

Sara shook her head in disbelief. "How fucking warped is that? If he hadn't got involved with that loan shark in the first place... Jesus, you were both abducted because of his involvement with the loan shark, how were you to blame for that?"

"I know. I tried to reason with him and..." Carla pointed at her face. "This was the result. He needs help."

"You're not wrong there," the chief was quick to agree. "I'm going to call for backup to take him in."

"What? No, you can't do that. I'm sure he'll calm down once he regains consciousness. We'll be able to set him free then."

Sara glanced at the chief's shocked expression.

Price shook her head. "I'm sorry, Carla, it's time to admit what he is. Abusive people never change, not in my experience. Yes, I agree, he needs professional help for his anger issues, but I can't, no, I *won't*, allow him to get away with what happened here today. He needs to learn to respect women. His whole demeanour was one of hatred for the fairer sex, I saw that with my own eyes. And frankly, if you failed to see that side of him today then I pity you, love. Maybe you're in desperate need of counselling yourself."

"I... I'm sorry."

Sara approached Carla and hugged her. "The first step is to admit defeat, admit when you're wrong, Carla. Granted, he needs help to get some control back in his life. I also think the chief is right, you need help, too. It's not right that you should feel guilty for what's going on with him. It's as though he has brainwashed you into believing you're in the wrong and he's always right."

Tears slid down Carla's flushed cheeks. "I don't see that. All I see is a man crying out to be loved, and I love him, no matter how he treats me. He doesn't mean it, deep down, I know that, and he knows it, too."

Sara resisted the temptation to shake her by the shoulders to make her partner see sense. "We're going to take him in and charge him, Carla, how do you feel about that?"

"What? Charge him with what? What he did to me?"

"No. What he did to me. He assaulted a police officer, and you know what? I'm going to need you to speak up as a witness to the event. Will you do that for me?"

Carla hesitated and then slowly nodded as the reality hit home. "If I'm forced to. He was wrong to lash out at you."

"He was in the wrong for slapping you, abusing you in front of us and for what he's done before over the months. I bet if you lifted your top up, we'd see bruise upon bruise there, wouldn't we?"

Carla avoided eye contact, giving Sara the answer she needed.

"Jesus, where do you think all this is going to end? With you on a slab at the mortuary is my guess, and yet you still can't see it, can you?"

"No. It would never come to that. He loves me."

"Well, if that's his kind of love, you can stick it where the sun don't shine. I think we should leave you alone to contemplate how close we all came to being seriously injured by your boyfriend today. You think he would have stopped at throttling me? No, I doubt it. He would have turned on the chief next, and then, once he'd punished her, he would have come after you. My guess is that he would probably lose control pounding you to a pulp, mainly for getting him into bother with me and the chief, if that makes sense."

"There's no proof any of that would have happened. He lost control for a split second. He didn't lay a hand on either you or the chief."

Gobsmacked at the blatant lie, Sara threw her arms up in despair.

The chief pulled Sara out of the way, held Carla by the shoulders and shook her. "Fucking wake up and see him for what he is, Carla, and yes, that's an order. I reckon you're lucky to still be alive. Had you not been a tough copper, he would have killed you long ago. Stop making excuses for him. He's an outright abusive bastard, who gets a thrill out of controlling a copper, that's my take on the situation. Don't fall under his spell again. Stick to your guns. Come out fighting, you're better than this, love."

"But I…"

"Love him," Sara finished her sentence for her. "That isn't love, sweetheart. It's pity or maybe even guilt for what he's been through the last year or so, since his accident. Take my word for it, it's not love."

Carla clutched her hand to her chest and shook her head.

Sara could see the confusion running through her mind.

"I can't… I think you'd better go, the pair of you."

"If that's what you want." Sara shrugged and tugged on the chief's arm. "We're clearly not wanted here. It's obvious she's made her decision."

"Oh no. I can't give up on her, and you shouldn't either," Price said, shaking her head. She turned to face Carla again. "You're wrong about this—you need us, not him, Carla."

Carla gulped and spread her arms out wide. "Why do I have to choose? Why can't I have both?"

Sara pulled on the chief's arm again. "Let me. Carla, you're part of our family, we don't give up on each other. It's a different story if you want to push us away. We can't force you to do anything, but I'll tell you this, Gary is going to be punished for lashing out here today. In my mind, you should have reported him months ago. Look at all the advice you've given to the women you've come across over the years, who have found themselves in the same position, suffered domestic abuse. You're a fool for not taking your own advice, surely you can see that, can't you?"

Carla paused and glanced at Gary. He groaned; he was waking up. She started to move towards him, but Sara caught her arm and whispered, "Don't. Leave him, he's liable to be angry and lash out again."

"How can he do that with his hands in cuffs?" Carla retorted sharply. She unhooked her arm and raced over to where Gary was trying his best to sit upright.

"What hit me? Carla, why are these two still here? I want it to be you and me, babe. You and me against the world." He tried to move his hands but realised they were tethered behind his back. "What the fuck is going on here?"

Carla smiled and ran a hand over his cheek. "Do as they say and you'll be home in no time."

"I ain't going nowhere. They can't make me, can they?"

Carla nodded. "You shouldn't have attacked Sara, they've got you by the short and curlies."

"What? I didn't do anything. She pushed me into a corner. I love you, Carla. Take the cuffs off, love. Go on, you've got the key." He winked at Carla. "I'll make it worth your while, you know, later in the bedroom."

Carla's cheeks coloured up, and she stood upright and stared down at him. His brow wrinkled into a deep frown. Sara could tell he wasn't used to women retreating from his passionate suggestions.

Is she on the turn? Go on, Carla. Give it to him. Tell him what you bloody think of him.

But Carla didn't. She moved to the farthest end of the room and stared back at all three of them. "How long is the backup going to take?"

Sara fished out her mobile. "I'll chase them up. They should be here soon." She rang the station, and Jeff informed her the patrol car was only a few streets away. "They're imminent."

"Good. I want him out of my sight before I change my mind."

"What are you saying, bitch?" Gary bellowed, struggling to stand with his hands out of action.

A siren sounded, and Sara rushed to open the front door. She welcomed the two uniformed officers and advised them that Gary was liable to be feisty when they moved him. She wasn't wrong. The two burly officers helped Gary to his feet. He head-butted one of them and kicked out at the other.

"It's a shame you didn't bring a Taser with you," the chief yelled. "That would keep him in line. Get him out of here, boys."

"You can't arrest me. I've done nothing wrong. I'm lashing out now because you've got me cornered. Don't think you're going to get away with treating me like this. My solicitor will get me off, no fear of that, because I'm innocent. You women are all the same, you've banded together, made up a cock and bull story, lies about me."

"Don't even go there, Gary. A judge will take one look at Carla's face and body and soon realise what's been going on for the past few months. You should be ashamed of yourself," Sara shouted.

"Fuck off, Ramsey. You think you know all there is to know about relationships, you know nothing. We're all different. Carla needs guidance, that's all I've been giving her."

Sara dashed across the room and stood before him with her hands on her hips. "Guidance? Is that what you call knocking seven bells out of her?" She eyed him up and down and shook her head. "You're an utter disgrace." She then prodded his temple a few times. "And sick in the head if that's what you believe."

He smiled and then spat in her face. Somehow, she'd been expecting it.

Refusing to show any sign of disgust, she ordered, "Take him away, boys. Mind he doesn't trip up on the way out." Once the two uniformed coppers had left the room with their prisoner, she removed a tissue from the packet she kept in her inside pocket and wiped her face. "What a disgusting excuse for the human race he is. I'm glad you appear to have seen the light at last, Carla."

Her partner approached and hugged her. "I'm so sorry, Sara. How will you ever be able to forgive me?"

"You can start by rescinding your resignation." Sara pushed away and looked Carla in the eye. She grinned and Carla's barrier crumbled.

"I will. I'm so very sorry I've put you both through this."

The chief came forward and briefly hugged them both. "Right, my job here is done. I've succeeded in achieving my goal. Take the rest of the day off, Carla, have a rest. Gary will be kept overnight, we'll make sure of that. Come back to work in the morning, rejuvenated after a good night's sleep."

"Thanks, boss. I'll be too busy searching for somewhere to live," Carla admitted.

"If you need a room for a few weeks while you find something, you can always stay with me and Mark," Sara volunteered.

"I can? That would take the pressure off a little. I'm so grateful to you, Sara, especially after the way I've treated you the past few days."

Sara waved her apology away. "It's a good job I love you. I don't take that kind of crap from just anyone, you know. Right, we'd better get back to work. We have two cases that need solving."

"Again, I'm sorry for causing so much disruption. I'll up my game tomorrow when I'm back at work, I promise."

Withdrawing her keys, Sara slipped her front door key off the keyring. "Make yourself at home. I'll be back the usual time."

"What about Mark? Shouldn't you run this past him first?"

"Nope. He's a pussycat, always eager to please. He'll love having two women to fuss over."

Carla's head dipped. "You're so lucky to have him."

"That I know. One day, you'll be saying the same, Carla. Keep the faith. There are still some good men left in this world."

"Shame I haven't found one yet. All I seem to attract are needy bastards. Hey, thinking about it, maybe I should ditch the idea of ever meeting someone who loves me for me. I've heard that sometimes works."

"Yep, it happened to a good friend of mine. She's now happily married with four kids, last I heard."

Carla's eyes widened. "A tad OTT. Not sure I want to go down the having kids route just yet. Glad to hear your friend found happiness in the end."

"She's such a sweetheart. Too trusting in many ways. I can definitely see the comparisons between the two of you. Pack your bags and move into mine during the day. There's no telling how long we're going to be able to hold Gary, if he gets a solicitor involved. Just be aware of that fact."

"I'll go and pack now. I can't thank you enough for always sticking by me. And thank you to you also, Chief, for coming here to make sure I was all right. You two genuinely are the best."

"Nonsense. I was only ensuring our expensive training didn't go to waste, that's all. We're going to have to fly. Stay safe, Carla. See you back at work tomorrow."

"I'll be there. And thank you once again for believing in me and holding my job open."

The chief tilted her head. "It was touch and go there for a while. I personally thought you were going to side with him and kick us out."

Carla's cheeks reddened.

Sara tutted. "You were, weren't you?"

"I contemplated it for the minutest of seconds. Glad I saw the error of my ways."

They hugged again, and then Sara and Carol left the house. On the journey back they discussed how they should handle Gary.

"Do you think she's likely to bring charges against him?" the chief asked.

"I strongly think she will now. I believe he used the accident as an excuse. I might do some extra digging into his background, see if he's got anything prior showing up."

"Good idea. When we get back to the station, leave him to me. I'll interview him, you won't be able to do it anyway, not if the charges are related to him striking you. You get back to the investigation."

"Crap, I feel so guilty for veering off the investigation, you know, about the distraction, but Carla needed our help."

"She did. Have you thought about holding a press conference? I know it's early, but if there's someone in Hereford intent on abducting women, maybe we should make the public aware of the situation promptly."

Sara thought the suggestion over for a little while and then agreed. "You might be right. I don't tend to call on the media this early, but at present, we haven't got much else to go on. I'll give Jane Donaldson a call now, see if she can line something up for me either today or tomorrow." She removed her mobile from her pocket and dialled Jane's number. "Hi, Jane, it's DI Sara Ramsey. How are you fixed for a press conference this afternoon, or am I pushing my luck?"

"Oh, hi. Umm… it's a quarter to three, might be pushing the limits. It's urgent, I take it?"

"You could say that. I had it in mind to try to warn the women of Hereford to be vigilant after we've had a couple of abductions in the area."

"I see. Does it have to be all the media? What about just radio journalists?"

"I'm not sure. I think we should go all in. I'm prepared to wait until the morning if I have to."

"Leave it with me. I'll see what I can sort out and get back to you."

"Thanks, Jane." She ended the call and returned her phone to her pocket.

"What do you believe is going on?" the chief asked.

"No idea. In truth, I'm frustrated as hell because we've got very little to go on. All we really have is the CCTV footage from the pub where the latest victim works, and that material can be classed as dubious because her car is barely in the frame. Nothing concrete to hand as yet. I'm hoping the team will have something we can sink our teeth into when I get back. That's probably wishful thinking on my part, though."

The chief drew to a stop behind a black sports car at a red light. "What I wouldn't give for one of them. What's the betting he's going to race away from the lights? If he does, fancy a bit of fun?"

Sara laughed. "Crikey, you must be totally bored sitting behind your desk dealing with paperwork day in, day out. Go on, go for it."

The lights changed, and the chief prepared herself for the chase ahead, except the man was a model driver and adhered to the speed limit. Carol slapped the steering wheel. "Spoilsport."

Sara chuckled until tears sprang to her eyes. "You're a card. You need to get out more."

"Ha, no chance of that happening anytime soon. It's been good to get out with you today, even if we got into major bother in the process. I hope Carla lives up to her promise and moves in with you for a few weeks. By the way, that was kind of you to offer your home as a sanctuary. I sense she's going to need a lot of pampering in the near future. Will Mark be okay?"

"I think I understand him well enough to know the answer to that. I'll give him a call when we get back. We're almost there now."

"Not many men would want to get involved in a domestic situation, I can tell you."

Sara suddenly had second thoughts. Mark was so easy-going, she doubted if anything would rattle him, make him angry. If anything, she thought he was likely to fling a protective arm around Carla's shoulders and pamper her to within an inch of her life. "He'll be fine. Or should I say, I hope he's going to be fine with the arrangements." A sudden glimmer of doubt seeped into her mind.

4
---

*L*ibby had nipped home to get changed into something far more casual. She slipped on a pair of comfy linen trousers and a sleeveless top to begin with, but all the top had done was highlight the size of her biceps, not a look she intended to go for. Instead, she hauled on a T-shirt with longer sleeves than normal. She was due to meet her next victim at a property on the other side of town. Satisfied with her presentation, she left the house, hopped into her car and set off.

Her mind whirred, distracting her with her plan to the point she nearly rear-ended the car in front of her when it stopped to let a bunch of kids cross the road. *What the fuck? Let them wait, arsehole. You won't be so lucky next time! Where would you be then? Carless and probably admitted to hospital with several broken bones.*

She selected first gear and continued on her journey, eyeing the road up ahead for the opportunity to overtake the idiot in front of her. Time was running out, she was only a few streets away from the rendezvous point now.

Drawing up outside the property, which was for sale, she waited in the car until Brittany Dawson appeared. She didn't have to wait long. Brittany wore a smart suit, with a skirt finishing just above the knee, trimmed off with a nice, neat short jacket. Her blonde hair billowed in the summer breeze. She tussled with it as she left the car and tied it back into a ponytail using a band she removed from her wrist.

Libby watched her prey for several seconds until she disappeared into the house with the board up outside. It was one of those posh townhouses; Libby had always fancied having a peek inside. This was an ideal opportunity, she could kill two birds at the same time, so to speak.

Locking the car, she approached the house. She scanned the area around her, aware that most people would probably still be at work at that time of the day. The doorbell chimed a merry tune. She waited patiently on the front step.

After a few seconds had passed, Brittany eventually opened the door with a cheery smile and welcomed her into the smart home. "Hi, I'm Brittany. So pleased to meet you." She offered Libby her hand.

"I'm Sasha Dobbs. Nice to see you. Time is a bit tight, a family issue has cropped up that I need to deal with ASAP."

"That's a shame. Okay, let's begin the tour. As you probably know, these houses were built around ten years ago."

"Yes, I've had my eye on them for a while. I'm intrigued to see how the inside is laid out. It's the three levels that has put me off viewing a property of this nature in the past."

"It's the same for most people. This style of living takes a lot of getting used to. I have friends who own townhouses, and they wouldn't dream of having anything else nowadays, because it offers so much flexibility. Let me show you what I mean. On this level we have a kitchen-diner, with a utility room off to the left, which includes a back door that leads out to the garden. Shall we take a look at that later?"

"Yes, okay. Seems a good-sized kitchen." She peered out of the large window at the postage stamp of a garden, unimpressed, but didn't voice her opinion.

Brittany led her up the first flight of stairs to the lounge on the right. "It's lovely having the lounge on a different level, don't you think?"

"Hmm… it's definitely large enough, although it might take some getting used to. Something I'll need to consider."

Brittany seemed offended by the comment. "You did view the property particulars before booking the appointment, didn't you?"

Libby frowned. "I did. Why?"

"It's just that we always put a floor plan on our particulars as a guide for what to expect."

"I saw that. But I was still intrigued enough to want to come for a look. If you think I'm wasting your time, why don't you come out and say it, bitch?"

Brittany took a step back, her forced smile disintegrating in an instant. "I beg your pardon? How dare you call me that?"

"You need to stop being so far up your own arse and speak to prospective customers with respect then." She ended her scornful comment with a slap.

Brittany appeared stunned by the assault. "What the hell did you do that for?"

"Because I wanted to. People like you need to be put in their place every now and again. I volunteered to be the one to do it in your case."

"I think we're done here. I need you to leave this house. Now."

"Or? And if I refuse? What do you intend to do about it?"

"I'll… I'll…," Brittany blustered, seemingly lost for words.

Libby watched her carefully, aware of any movement she might make to reach for her mobile. "Let's continue the tour, see what you're made of, whether you can turn this doubter into a prospective buyer."

"No. I refuse to. I've asked you to leave this house. I'm through with being nice to you. You've treated me disrespectfully; I no longer have to be courteous to you. You've made it perfectly clear that you have no intention of buying this property, therefore, I must insist that we end this tour. I have other clients to see, people who aren't time-wasters."

Libby glared at her and took a few steps closer. "I said I want to finish this shitty tour—either you continue or suffer the consequences."

"What the hell are you talking about? Is that some kind of threat?"

"A threat that I will make good on unless you get on with the tour.

79

What's through here?" Libby went into the hallway and waited for Brittany to join her.

The estate agent slipped her hand into her jacket pocket. Libby was quick to react. She grabbed Brittany's arm and yanked on it. Brittany's mobile tumbled to the floor. On the screen were two nines.

"About to call the police, were you?" She lashed out, swiped the estate agent around the face. Hard enough to leave a handprint on her pale cheek.

"Please don't hit me again. Who are you, what do you want from me?"

"You're not in a position to tell me what I can and can't do, got that? Now, resume the tour."

Hesitantly, Brittany opened the door to the next room off the hallway. "This is the main bathroom."

"It's not."

"It's not what?" Brittany asked, confused.

"A bathroom. It's a shower room."

Brittany let out a deep sigh. "Of course it is. Silly me."

"Stop trying to dupe me, you'll fail. I'm much, much smarter than you, you'll find that out later."

Frowning Brittany paused. "Meaning?"

"Meaning, get back on track. Speak to me properly, like the best client you've ever dealt with, or there will be a cost involved if you don't."

Brittany gulped and pulled at her ponytail then ventured on with the tour. "Okay. This is a double bedroom, and that concludes the rooms on this floor." She gestured for Libby to ascend the stairs up to the final level ahead of her.

Libby waved a finger. "Not likely. After you."

Brittany rolled her eyes and started up the stairs. They were halfway up when she kicked a leg behind her. Her heel caught Libby in the face and sent her tumbling backwards.

"Why you..." Libby raced back up the stairs, two at a time, after the screaming Brittany.

Libby knew she had to be quick, to prevent the woman from

locking herself in one of the rooms ahead. She dived at her ankles and brought the estate agent down. Brittany kicked out and screamed. Libby got to her feet, kicked the woman in the stomach a couple of times and then slouched against the wall to take stock of what she'd been forced to do. It hadn't been her intention to hurt any of the women, not really. But Brittany had pushed her to her limits, and she'd snapped. Vile creature that she was. She hadn't changed over the years, not one iota.

"Please let me go. I didn't mean to hurt you, I'm scared, surely you can see that."

"I can. And believe me when I say this, you have every right to be scared. I've waited a long time to get revenge. You and the others will regret the day…"

"The day? Do I know you? I don't recognise you. Tell me what I've done. Let me make it up to you. Please, I don't want to be in this situation. I've only just got married."

Libby inclined her head. "What's that got to do with anything?"

"I…"

One look from Libby put a stop to Brittany's whining. Her full red lips twisted out of shape, and tears surfaced in her eyes.

Libby shook her head. "Excuses don't wash with me, just so you know."

Libby then thumped her hard in the face. Brittany didn't see the strike coming and sank heavily onto the thick carpet.

In one easy movement, Libby hitched Brittany onto her shoulder and carried her down the two flights of stairs. She placed her against the front door, one hand at her chest holding her upright, and peered out. After making sure she wasn't likely to be challenged by one of the neighbours, Libby made her move. Ensuring the front door was secured behind her, she hooked Brittany's arm around her shoulder and half dragged her to the car. Any onlookers would have thought Brittany had passed out and Libby was just being a Good Samaritan, assisting her to her car. She placed the woman in the back seat, slammed the door shut and drove to a local beauty spot she knew a few streets away.

There, thankful that there were no other cars in sight, she got out of the vehicle, yanked Brittany out and shoved her in the boot, just in case she regained consciousness during the drive back—less dangerous that way. Libby returned to the car and drove back to the lockup. She had a busy day looming, and time was of the essence in order to fulfil her plans. There, she heaved Brittany's body out of the boot, hoisted her slender frame onto her shoulders and carried her through the building to her designated cell.

"Hello, who's there? Please help us. Please let us go," came the cries from Jennifer and Amanda.

Libby suppressed a giggle and left the lockup again. She had enough time to get home before she had to pick up her fourth victim at around five-forty-five. She smiled at the thought and drove back to the house. All the time wondering if the women had introduced themselves back at their temporary prison and if they'd had the brains to figure out what was going on yet. She doubted it. They had always been self-consumed, shallow individuals during the time she'd known them.

They aren't so brave now, though, are they? Only a few more hours and the fun can begin. I'm going to enjoy what lies ahead of them, however, I doubt they will.

5

$\mathcal{S}$ara left the chief to deal with Gary and returned to the incident room to catch up on her team's progress. There really wasn't much to hand, which was another cause of frustration for her.

In need of caffeine, she stopped off at the machine, bought the rest of the team a drink and asked Craig to hand them around. Then she went into her office and rang Mark.

"Hello, you. Everything all right?" he asked, ever intuitive.

"Not really." She briefly recapped how her day had panned out so far with regard to Carla.

"Jesus. What is wrong with these men, abusing their partners like that? Hey, if she needs somewhere to stay while she finds other accommodation, don't hesitate offering her our spare room."

She smiled. He truly was the most kind and considerate man she knew, apart from her father and her neighbour, Ted. It gladdened her heart to know there were men out there who still treated women as equals. It balanced things out, made up for those who preferred to knock women down at every given opportunity. "You're so sweet. I'm glad you said that. I told her the same. I've given her my key. I was ringing up to pre-warn you, in case you got home early tonight.

Umm… try not to react when you see the state of her, she's far from her usual beautiful self at present."

He let out a large sigh. "That's going to upset me, seeing her all battered and bruised."

"I know it will, which is why I wanted to warn you, love. Anyway, how has your day been?"

"Not bad so far. I should be home relatively early this evening. I'll stop off and pick up a couple of bottles of wine on the way, shall I?"

"Would you mind? I'll pay you when I get home. I might be a little late, depends if I have to do a conference tonight, or not before I leave. I need to chase Jane up after I've finished speaking to you."

"Hey, you go. We can chat later."

"Thanks, Mark, you're such a sweetheart. I never have to consider what it was that made me fall in love with you."

"You say the nicest things. We're two of a kind, Sara. Don't ever forget how much I love you."

"I won't. I treasure every minute of the day I spend with you. Too gushy, right? I'm going now."

He laughed. "Maybe a touch. See you later, darling."

She ended the call and chased up Jane right away.

"Hey, I was about to call you. I couldn't manage to cobble things together for this afternoon, so I've gone full hog for tomorrow morning at ten, how's that?"

"Brilliant. You're amazing, but then I always end up giving you praise on a job well done, don't I?"

"You do. It's my job, Sara. Sorry I couldn't deliver for this afternoon. This way, at least you can have some extra time to prepare what you want to say. That's not always the case, is it?"

"Too true. Thanks, Jane. Have a good evening, I'll see you in the morning, around nine-fifty?"

"I'll be there. Take care, Sara."

She hung up, finished off her coffee which was on the verge of going cold and joined the team again.

"I was about to come and see you, boss," Craig said, crossing the room towards her.

"Sounds ominous. What have you got for me?"

"Uniform have reported they've located Jennifer Moore's car. I've arranged for someone from the lab to pick it up. I hope I have done the right thing, boss?"

"You have. That's great news, where was it found?"

"This is the strange part: outside a house which can only be described as derelict. Which is probably why our guys haven't managed to locate it until now."

"Very strange. Let's see what SOCO can find, hopefully it'll help us. God knows we could do with the assistance on this one. Anything else?"

Christine raised her hand, and Sara walked over to her desk. "What have you got?"

"I've been checking into the women's social media accounts. I have an association with them through Facebook."

"An association? Can you clarify what you mean?"

"Sorry, yes, they're on each other's friends' list but nothing more than that. I've scrolled back through several months of posts. They're both quite active on the site, and my assumption would be they're not really that close."

"How odd." Sara paused and thought things over for a moment or two. "What about schools, they're of a similar age, aren't they? Did they go to the same school? Maybe that's the connection here."

"Let me have a look at their profiles. Hang on, Charlesworth School for Jennifer, and yes, the same for Amanda."

"Okay, let's add that to the board. It might come in handy later. At least it's a step in the right direction. I'm fed up with going backwards all the time. I much prefer it when the information we gather drives an investigation forward."

"I agree, boss. Can I ask what happened with Carla?" Christine asked.

"Sorry, yes. You guys should know that the chief and I visited Carla to try to persuade her to rethink her resignation. Whilst we were chatting, Gary came home."

Christine winced.

Sara nodded. "Yep, it wasn't pleasant. He's downstairs being questioned by the chief now. He assaulted me." She waved away the gasps. "I'm fine. Carla finally saw what he was like. She's left him and will be staying with me until she finds alternative accommodation."

"Excellent news. You didn't have to do that, boss," Christine replied.

"I know. I couldn't see her on the streets. It won't be for long. Hopefully, being out of his clutches will make her regain some of her confidence. Upon reflection, I believe she's been lacking in that department for a while."

"What's this?" a voice sounded behind her.

She spun around to find DI Des Williams from Worcester standing in the doorway. He had been the one called in to take over the previous case when it had led to Carla and Gary being abducted, although the investigation they had been working on hadn't really been connected in the end.

"Hey, stranger, what are you doing here?" Sara stepped forward and hugged him. Even though she hadn't got on well with him initially, being an outsider, she'd come to think of him as a friend in the end. "Wait, let me grab a couple of coffees, you can tell me all the gossip in my office."

"How could I refuse such a tempting offer? White with one for me, in case you've forgotten."

"Cheeky, I hadn't. I made enough of them while you were with us last month."

Coffees bought, they went through to the office.

Once they were both settled into their seats, Sara asked, "What are you doing in our neck of the woods again, so soon?"

"You avoided answering my question, we'll get back to that one in a sec. I've been called in to assist another team with a gang-related issue. Some of the action has taken place on my patch, so we've agreed to work together to try and trap the buggers. Should be fun. You'll be seeing more of me over the next couple of weeks. Back to my question." He grinned, persistent as always.

"You never let anything drop, do you? Okay, this is between you and me, I'm counting on your discretion here."

"You've got it. Before you say anything else, I noticed that Carla was missing. Is there a connection? Were you talking about her?"

"You're very astute, for a copper." Sara laughed. "She's got herself in a mess, but we're sorting it now."

"What sort of mess? Does this have something to do with her boyfriend? The one who was abducted?"

"Yes." Sara went on to explain what Carla had been dealing with over the last few months. She watched his expressions change from concern to anger and back to concern, all in the space of five minutes.

"What the actual fuck? Sorry, excuse my language. I hate it when I hear accounts like this, especially against a fellow officer. What gives a bloke the right to hit a woman in the first place? Let alone a serving police officer. He must be dense if he thought he'd get away with it."

Sara hitched up a shoulder. "The problem is, he *did* almost get away with it. She handed in her resignation. If it hadn't been for our DCI visiting her, and then hauling my arse round there to talk some sense into Carla, I think he would have succeeded. The idiot ended up assaulting me. That proved to be his downfall and made Carla realise just who she was involved with."

"Sounds to me like she's had a lucky escape. Where is she now?"

"In the process of moving her stuff into my house. I've told her she can have our spare room for a few weeks until she finds alternative accommodation. She seemed relieved by the offer."

"I'm not surprised. What about her family?"

Sara paused to think. "She doesn't really speak about them much. Only in passing. God, what kind of partner am I? I don't even know her mum's and dad's names or where they live. It's never really cropped up, and yet, she knows everything about my family. Shame on me."

"Don't do that. I'm sure there's a reason why she hasn't told you. Maybe she's ashamed of them."

"What? Why?"

He shrugged. "I have no idea. Something to discuss in the future. Being her superior, you have access to her personnel file, don't you?"

"Hmm... if I snooped, I'd feel I was intruding on her privacy."

He wrinkled his nose. "Forget I mentioned it. How was she when you left her?"

"Apart from the dozens of bruises she's sporting, she seemed to be okay. Possibly relieved it was over. Who knows what she'll feel like this evening once she's had the chance to reflect on how things turned out? I know she feels guilty about involving me."

"That's understandable. You're a kind person, you know, to offer her a place to stay."

"You'd do the same, wouldn't you?"

He shifted in his chair. "Umm... not sure that would have come across too well."

"You being a man, you mean? Or is there something else you're not telling me?" Sara's eyes narrowed, and she gasped. "Jesus, I can see it written all over your face. You bloody fancy her, don't you? Go on, make my day and admit it."

The colour appeared in his neck and quickly gained momentum to settle in his cheeks.

Sara smiled and sat back.

"Do you have to be so smug?"

She laughed. "I love being right, it's true. Want me to have a word with her?"

"Pack it in. After what she's bloody been through, it wouldn't surprise me if she ended up hating men and being turned off us for life."

Sara shook her head. "Bollocks, she enjoys sex too much. Oops... too much information, right?"

He placed a hand over his eyes, dropped it and reached for his drink. "You're, what's the word...?"

"Amazing? The best DI to ever walk the earth?"

"Nope, incorrigible, that's the word I was seeking."

They both laughed.

"Joking aside, I think you'd make a fabulous couple. Two good-looking specimens such as yourselves, I can visualise what beautiful children you'd produce."

"Jesus Christ… slow down, woman. In five minutes flat, you've gone from trying to set us up on a date, to marrying us off and having bundles of joy, or ankle biters. Give me a break."

"Hey, let's face it, neither of you is getting any younger, and her body clock is ticking, if you get my meaning."

He covered his eyes again, the smile twitching at his lips as he considered her suggestion.

"Enough. This conversation remains between us, right? If I hear you've been spouting your mouth off, I'll…"

"You'll what? Thank me for intervening? I thought so."

"You're bloody unbelievable. How does your fella put up with you?"

There was a knock on the door, and both of them fell quiet, aware of the subject they'd been discussing.

"Come in," Sara shouted.

Marissa poked her head into the room. "Sorry to interrupt, boss. I thought you should know straight away."

"Know what?"

"We've received a call from an estate agency manager in town who has reported one of their female agents missing."

Sara shot out of her chair. "Sorry, Des, you don't mind, do you? It could be relevant to the investigations we're working on at present."

"Go ahead. I've stayed longer than anticipated anyway." He rose from his chair and followed Sara out of the office. He patted her on the back and said, "Good luck."

"Thanks, you, too. Stay in touch. We should go for a drink after work one day."

He rolled his eyes, picking up on her inference. "We'll see. Take care."

"Ditto." She turned her back on him and asked Marissa for the details.

"I've got the phone number. It's Jackson's in town. I've told the manager that you'll be in touch soon."

"I'll drop over there now, it's not like I'm doing anything else. Craig, come with me."

Marissa handed her a note with the address on, and they set off.

During the trip, Craig said, "Nice to see DI Williams again."

"It was. He's helping out on a gang-related case which covers Worcester and Hereford."

"Interesting. He seems a decent chap."

"He does," Sara agreed, unsure where Craig was heading. "Something you want to say, Craig?"

He slapped a hand to his chest. "Me? No. Genuinely interested in what's going on around me, that's all, boss."

"A probing mind we call it. Either that or you're nosey."

"Charming. I prefer to think of it as the former."

They reached the estate agency ten minutes later and parked in the only available space in the car park. Sara locked her vehicle, and they entered the office via the main entrance. Three females were sitting at the desks, two of them on the phone.

The redhead who was free approached them. "Hello, can I help?"

Sara produced her warrant card. "I'm DI Sara Ramsey, and this is my partner, DC Craig Watson."

"Oh, thank goodness you've taken my call seriously. I've been fraught with bloody worry."

"Sorry, I didn't catch your name."

"It's Miranda Richards. I'm the branch manager. I've never been under this much stress before."

"Okay, try and remain calm. Is there somewhere we can talk without being disturbed?"

"Yes, my office. Come through. I didn't want to be alone so sat out there with Shell and Jackie. I feel a lot calmer than I did when I made the call to the station."

They each took a chair in the large windowless office. It felt stuffy to Sara, she hated not being able to browse out of the window during the day. She was lucky, back at the station, to have magnificent views of the Brecon Beacons to brighten her working day, unlike Miranda Richards.

"Mrs Richards, perhaps you can run through what happened?"

"It's Brittany Dawson, one of our top negotiators, she's gone missing. And before you say it, yes, I've tried ringing her phone and I've also tried my best to contact the person she was due to meet."

"I take it you've been unsuccessful with both?"

"Yes. I didn't know what to do next so I rang the police in the hope you could offer me some advice. After the Suzy Lamplugh case, well, we were all instructed to change our systems."

"And that's worked out for you up until now, I take it?"

"Yes. Oh God... please, we're wasting time. You have to put out a bulletin to say she's missing. Get every available police car and officer on the alert for her. I can't bear to think of anything awful happening to her. I'd feel so guilty if something were to go wrong and she got hurt." The woman's shaking hand swept back a stray hair that had slipped out of the French knot.

"Please try not to worry. We're going to do our utmost to find Brittany. We'll need the address of the property where the viewing took place and the name of the person she had the appointment with."

"It was a townhouse in Winchester Avenue, and the woman she was due to meet there was a Sasha Dobbs who contacted us this week. We rang her back on her mobile and got all her details."

"Can I see them?"

"Of course. I have them to hand, obviously. I've tried calling her number every ten minutes or so. The phone is dead."

Sara nodded and slid the sheet of paper with the number on it in Craig's direction. "Try it again, for me, Constable."

"We should have done the thorough checks, admittedly, but we've been under a lot of pressure. Two of my girls are off work, one with malaria, and Jody is still on maternity leave. Brittany assured me she felt comfortable with the woman every time she spoke to her over the phone, and I was satisfied with her decision. And now this... Please, you have to bring her back to us safely, you hear of so many frightful things happening to young women these days. Women getting killed by deranged individuals. Oh God, did I say that? I shouldn't be talking such rubbish out loud."

"It's okay. You've done the right thing by contacting us quickly. We're on the case now. We're going to give it our all to bring her home, I promise you. I need to know if Brittany has had any problems lately."

"In what respect?" Miranda dabbed a tissue under her eyes to catch the tears as they fell.

"Has she argued with anyone, perhaps here or maybe on the street, another shop owner or something along those lines?"

"Now you've mentioned it… just the other day she had a problem parking her car out back when the guy next door, in the off-licence, refused to move his car. It was blocking our entrance. Bloody idiot, he is. Always playing the big I am, flashy car that matches his smile."

"What sort of problem? How did it manifest?"

"He mainly shouted at her. I went out there to try to calm things down a bit. Rude man, he told us to F off. I pulled Brittany away, insisted she should ignore him."

"Did he make any threats?"

"Not outright, but the inference was there, if you get my drift?"

"I do. Okay, we'll stop by and have a word with him. What about strange viewings or calls that you've thought a little weird, anything there?"

"No, nothing since last year. A man kept booking appointments with Jody when she first found out she was pregnant. It made her feel uncomfortable, so I stepped in on one of the appointments. By that I mean, we both showed up at the viewing. He got the message and hasn't contacted the branch since. I got the impression he was harmless enough, just took a fancy to Jody. Ordinarily, I think she would have brushed it off, but her hormones were raging and heightened the issue for her."

"All right. I don't suppose you can remember his name? If you have his address, even better. We can run his details through our system, just in case."

"That makes sense. But take on board that he hasn't been around for months, more than that, maybe over a year. I don't think he's likely to be involved, do you?"

"Stranger things have happened. Answer me this, are you in contact with the other estate agents?"

"Yes, of course. We might be in competition with each other but we still look out for one another."

"You mean if there's a problem with a client you help to spread the word?"

"Exactly. There's like an unspoken code between us."

"Glad to hear it."

Miranda pushed back her chair and stood. "Let me get the man's details for you. I think I can roughly remember his name."

"That'll be great."

"I'm going to check with my staff, if that's all right."

Sara nodded, and Miranda left the office.

"Do you really think it's worth interviewing the bloke next door?" Craig asked.

"What makes you say that?" she replied, intrigued as to what he was getting at.

"I might be speaking out of turn here but I thought we were looking for a female suspect. Everything we've gathered so far is pointing in that direction."

"Possibly. Although we can't rule out a couple being involved."

He tutted. "You're right, of course. Forget I spoke."

Sara tapped his knee. "Don't ever apologise for raising a query, Craig."

He smiled.

Miranda wandered back into the room and handed Sara a slip of paper. "His details. Cameron Stitch. His address is there. Of course, there's always a possibility he has moved since he was registered with us. Maybe he was a genuine buyer and found a suitable property elsewhere."

"Maybe the jungle drums might know?" Sara asked, hoping the woman would make some calls for her to save them time back at the station.

"I could ring the other agencies, if you want me to."

"Perfect. Every bit of help we can get at this stage is a bonus. Why don't we go next door, have a word with your rude neighbour and drop back to see you again in a few minutes?"

"Sounds good to me." Miranda picked up her phone while Sara and Craig left the office.

They nipped next door and asked to speak to the manager. The young male assistant went in search of his boss and returned with a tall man in his thirties, his hair gelled back. His suit had a designer look about it, and his shoes shone brightly under the shop lights.

"Hello, I'm the manager. How may I help?"

Sara produced her ID and introduced herself and Craig. "Sorry, I missed your name, sir."

"It's David Davidson, am I in trouble?"

"We're led to believe you had a run-in with the ladies next door recently."

"Is it a crime to have words with someone nowadays? I wasn't aware of that."

Sara found his response laced with sarcasm and took an instant dislike to him.

"It is when the person you had an argument with has been reported missing," Sara retorted, her gaze locked with his.

Davidson's eyes widened. "What? And you believe I have something to do with her disappearance? Are you crazy?"

"Maybe. Where were you at lunchtime today?"

"Here. I haven't left the shop all day. It's ordering day. You can ask my two members of staff." He pointed at the young man who had returned behind the counter. "This is Steve, and Adam is out back counting the stock with me."

"We'll do that in a moment. Why did you feel the need to have a go at Brittany Dawson?"

"Because she lacked patience. Those women are all the same. In and out of that damn car park all day, our paths are bound to cross at times and hold-ups are bound to happen. Some people tend to deal with them better than others. She always flies off the handle, that one. I'm sorry she's gone missing, though. I take it that occurred today?"

"Yes. I don't suppose you've seen anyone suspicious hanging around in the past few days?"

"No. Not that I've noticed. I really don't know what else I can tell you. You can take my word that I had nothing to do with it."

Sara got the impression she was wasting her time. She asked to verify Davidson's account of his whereabouts with his staff, which they did, and then she and Craig returned to see if Miranda had further news for them.

"Any luck next door?" Miranda asked.

They had rejoined the woman in the office and sat opposite her. "No joy. I could tell by his reaction he didn't know Brittany was missing. How did you get on?"

"I rang several of the other agencies, and they checked their systems. They all had him on their books, so maybe we misread his intentions at the time. My friend at Spooner's told me she sold him a detached property not long after I showed up on that last viewing with him."

"Interesting. I don't suppose you got his address from your friend?"

"I did. I explained the situation, and she was only too willing to hand it over, with the caveat that you didn't get the information from her."

"Agreed. Thanks for your help." Leaving with the information, Sara drove back to the station and set the team digging into Cameron Stitch's background. Nothing came to light on the man, so they quickly put him aside as a suspect. Likewise with David Davidson. Sara just didn't get a bad feeling about the man, and the shocked reaction she'd received from him, once he heard Brittany was missing, was enough to put her mind at ease. Therefore, they found themselves back to square one. The only difference to this morning was that there were now three women missing instead of two.

6

*A*fter changing her clothes and eating a swift sandwich to keep her energy levels high, Libby jumped back in her Golf and set off for the next location. Ashleigh Calder, her next victim, was waiting.

She arrived too early and, knowing the woman's routine well, she drove around the block a few times and then parked in one of the bays at the rear of the boutique, next to Ashleigh's convertible Merc. What she wouldn't give to own a car like that. Maybe she could force the woman to part with the keys and sign the log book over to her, once the games began. Ashleigh's boutique was the place to go if you or your fella had deep pockets. Libby had never set foot in the shop but had checked out the prices online, and they were astronomical. *No wonder she can afford to drive around in an expensive car.*

Her gaze zeroed in on the back door to the shop. Even that was nicely presented with a hanging basket full of beautiful blooms, positioned on either side of the door. To anyone else, the expenditure would be classed as a waste of money, but not to Ashleigh. When Libby had visited and put Ashleigh under surveillance, the woman lovingly tended to the plants every day. Watering the baskets, feeding them when necessary, to maintain and, possibly, prolong their blooms.

She swapped seats, made herself comfortable and sat low in her seat, in case Ashleigh was watching her from inside. She doubted it, but she thought it would be better to err on the side of caution, nevertheless.

Finally, after ten minutes of Libby sitting with a kink in her back, Ashleigh appeared. She tweaked the baskets, deadheading a couple of the flowers and placing the faded ones in the bin to her right. The next second, she was heading towards the Merc. Libby prepared herself. She would need to overpower the woman swiftly, and from what she could remember from their schooldays, Ashleigh never did anything without going down with a fight first.

Libby had something special at her disposal to combat any anticipated trouble. The can was in her right hand and, with her left, she opened the passenger door of the Golf. Ashleigh glanced up in surprise and unbelievably recognised her.

"You. What are you doing here?"

Libby gulped, her tough exterior taking a hit under Ashleigh's piercing stare. She panicked, knew if she didn't react quickly the opportunity would pass her by and her plan would be shattered into a gazillion pieces. *Do it! I have to do it, now!*

Aiming the can, she pressed the top, and the spray hit Ashleigh full in the face. The woman screamed. Libby had to act fast. To shut her up before someone came to her rescue. She belted Ashleigh in the face a couple of times. Ashleigh grunted and dropped to the ground, however, before Libby had the chance to bind her or pounce on her to subdue her in another way, Ashleigh bounced back onto her feet and took up a combat stance, her hands slanted, ready to attack karate style.

Libby wasn't fooled, she'd done her homework on Ashleigh, on all of them. She was aware that Ashleigh had attended a local karate class only the once and decided to never return, after not being able to hack it, Libby guessed. Libby engaged the woman in a karate stance of her own and watched the confusion rise in Ashleigh's face, her eyes watering and constantly blinking from the effects of the pepper spray.

"Give it up, I know you bailed out after only one lesson, unlike me. Come willingly, and I'll go easy on you. If you choose to put up a fight... well, let's just say you'd be foolish to entertain doing that."

"What do you want? It's been years since we last met. I barely recognised you."

"Unlike the others. They're still none the wiser."

"What? Are you telling me you've seen the others?"

"Oh yes. They're all safely confined in a special place. You'll be joining them soon."

"I bloody won't." Ashleigh turned and legged it, screaming furiously as she ran.

Libby jumped on her back and beat her to the ground, silencing her cries for help with every blow. Finally, Ashleigh lay still beneath her. She needed to act rapidly, to get Ashleigh in the car before someone appeared to try to help her. The woman was slight but heavier than the others because she was a few inches taller and had obviously built up her muscle mass through exercise. Libby was intrigued to know how that snippet of information would present itself when the games began. A thrill of excitement travelled down her spine. After a couple of attempts, which involved different stances, she managed to lift Ashleigh and drop her in the boot of her car. Keen to get back, she drove at speed to the lockup and unloaded her latest acquisition. Whilst Libby carried Ashleigh through the building, she woke up and lashed out with her arms and legs, forcing Libby to drop her on the floor. Ashleigh squirmed back against the wall and used it to help herself get to her feet. One look into her eyes and Libby could tell Ashleigh was still in a daze and possibly too groggy to put up much of a fight.

"Come on then, tiger, let me have it. You know you want to, it's whether you've got it in you to take me on. In case you hadn't noticed, I have the strength and determination of a charging rhinoceros. So bring it on!"

"I don't want this. I just want to go home. Why are you doing this?"

"Guess! You and the others need to be taught a lesson. You took great pleasure in making my life hell once upon a time. Well, let's just say that Sleeping Beauty has now woken up and is determined to right the wrongs of her past."

"I'm sorry. I'm sure the others are, too. Are they here?" Ashleigh glanced down the long corridor.

"Yes, they're here. Isn't it nice? You all being back together again? Except this time, I'm the one in control, not you."

"What are you talking about? What do you intend doing to us?"

Libby laughed and tipped her head back. "All these questions are futile. When the time is right, the games will begin. I can't wait for it to happen either. Matching you against... no, I'll stop there. Let you stew on that for a while. We're going to have a blast together. Maybe not for some of you; in the end, it's going to come down to the survival of the fittest." She leaned in and winked at Ashleigh. "My money is on you being the triumphant one, the victor if you will. You have the strength of character to succeed. I can also tell you work out as well. Don't let me down, Ashleigh, will you?"

Ashleigh refused to respond. Her gaze travelled the length of the hallway again. "What's down there?" There was a tremor to her voice that sent a satisfying thrill through Libby.

"You'll find out when the time is right. Now, are you going to cooperate and walk on your own two feet or do I have to knock you out again?"

"No. I think I can manage to walk. Please don't hurt me."

"Good. Let's go." Libby tugged at Ashleigh's elbow.

The woman resisted at first until Libby glared at her.

It was a painstakingly long journey. Libby gave Ashleigh the benefit of the doubt, putting her intrinsically slow speed down to the fuzziness in her head.

"Come on, try and up your pace. It'll be dark soon."

Ashleigh looked at her as if she belonged on a psych ward. "Are you kidding me? There are no windows in here, what does it matter what's going on outside?"

Libby winked. "Nice to see there's nothing wrong with your observational skills. This way, only a few steps more."

The outer door was firmly shut. Libby kept one eye on Ashleigh, who she'd placed beside her, as she opened the door that led to the cells. "In here. This one has your name written on it."

"Help! Let me out of here! Please, I don't want to be here. Help me!"

"I don't want to be here either. Please, let us go!"

"Nor me. I echo what the others have said. Let us go, please."

The three occupants took it in turns to cry out. Libby shoved Ashleigh into her cell and guided her to the thin mattress. She pointed out the essentials in the confined space along with their uses and left. Libby checked Ashleigh's demeanour through the spyhole. She was downcast at best, her feistiness now a thing of the past. After ensuring Ashleigh was okay, she peered into the other cells to observe the women. All of them shrank back under her gaze. Once she'd checked on them, she stood in the middle of the room and shouted, "Rest now, my beauties. I will return in a few hours. The games will begin then, now there are four of you. It would be ideal if you were all here, but time hasn't been on my side lately. The fifth one will join you shortly, I promise. Until then, we'll have some fun getting to know each other again."

She slammed the outer door shut and stood back against the wall, pretending she'd left the women alone.

Ashleigh was the first to speak. "Hello, I'm Ashleigh Calder. Who are you, and do you know what she wants from us?"

"Ashleigh, is that really you? This is Jennifer Moore, my maiden name was Sims."

"My God. Have you been here long?"

"A few days. More time than I care to remember. I don't know who she is. Do you?"

"I know her but I've forgotten her name. She's spoken about revenge. Has anything happened yet?"

"No, nothing. The others are here. Introduce yourselves, girls. It's good to be back together again. We'll be stronger as a group, I'm sure we will."

"You reckon," Ashleigh grumbled.

"I'm here. Amanda Smith."

"Hi, Amanda. How are you? Don't answer that, it was a frigging dumb question. Is Nicole here?"

"No. I don't think so," Jennifer replied.

"I'm here, you'd remember me as Brit Mitchell. I'm married now. Oh shit, I hope I get to see my husband again. I love him so much."

"You will. It's imperative that we remain positive at all times. We can get through this together," Jennifer assured the rest of the group.

"I'm not so sure. She mentioned something about the games beginning later. What could she mean? I get the feeling she wasn't talking about playing Monopoly," Ashleigh replied.

Libby could no longer hold the laughter in. She roared and applauded at the same time. "Bravo, ladies. Has it sunk in yet? Who am I?"

None of them responded through the sudden quiet and stillness.

"One of life's mysteries yet to be answered, right? We met back in the day when puberty was changing our bodies, in some cases, for the worse. I'll leave you with that thought and return later. TTFN, bitches." She slammed the door behind her and returned to her car with the intention of going home for a couple of hours' nap. Her day's exploits had drained her. She needed to recover for what lay ahead that evening. Excitement took over as the adrenaline pumped around her system.

7

Sara arrived home and rang the bell. She knew Carla was already there, her car was sitting on the road outside. A strange sensation shot through her, and she put it down to knowing that her partner and friend was safe, at last.

Carla opened the front door with a contented-sounding Misty in her arms. "Sorry, I wasn't sure if I should leave it unlocked for you or not."

"It's fine. I'd rather you didn't. I'm very security-minded after what this one went through." She stroked Misty, who was revelling in all the fuss being heaped upon her.

"Ah yes, I should have thought about that. Want a coffee? Is that correct protocol? To ask you if you want a drink in your own home? I'm not sure."

"Don't be daft. It's your home now, if only temporarily, and yes, I'd love one."

Carla handed Misty over and sped into the kitchen. "If you tell me what veggies you need preparing for dinner, I can get on with them for you."

"Gosh, I'm not that well organised. Mark tends to do most of the cooking. I'll give him a call, see if he's got anything planned for this evening. Sometimes he'll stop off for a takeaway if we're both up to our necks in work and exhausted, which suits me."

"Want me to check the fridge first? Maybe we can surprise him with something home-cooked for a change." Carla winked and smiled.

"Cheeky mare. I do cook some days, admittedly it's mostly at the weekend."

"Just teasing." Carla finished making the coffee. "Here, take the weight off and drink that." Then she opened the fridge and shifted a few things around. Once or twice, she poked her head around the fridge door to look at Sara.

"Something wrong? Oh God, you haven't found anything sprouting young in there, have you?"

"Nearly. Found a few furry items." Carla pulled the dustbin closer and started filling it with food long past its 'eat by' date.

"Now you're making me feel bad."

"Oh no, that wasn't my intention. I'm only trying to help. I get days when I have to blitz my fridge as well, we all do."

"If you say so. Anything worth keeping in there? I could have a rummage around in the freezer; I might have a few portions of lasagne left. I do a batch cook now and then, mainly to use up the crap that's left before it gets relegated to the bin."

"Oo… I lurve lasagne. Stay there, I'll get it. Where am I likely to find it?"

"Top drawer in the freezer."

Carla bent down and opened the door. "Ah ha, my investigative nose has spotted two, no, three likely suspects. I think we're in luck. What do you usually serve with it?"

"That's a relief. Umm… it depends, sometimes chips, but mostly salad."

Carla turned back to the freezer and extracted the bag of chips. "This looks the likely option as the salad ingredients are a tad thin on the ground."

"Sounds good to me. We'll sort it later, let it thaw a little while we have a cuppa. Come and join me."

Carla set the food containers on the draining board, picked up her cup and joined Sara at the kitchen table. "Thanks again for letting me stay, Sara. I'll try not to get under your feet too much. If you and Mark want any privacy at any time, don't be afraid to tell me, will you?"

"I won't. Glad to see you've made yourself at home. How are you feeling about everything?"

"To be honest, I've done my best to try to keep busy since I got here. Misty has been a massive source of comfort. I never knew cats could be so entertaining, it's as if she knew I was crying out for affection."

Sara reached over and laid her hand on top of Carla's. "Bless you. You're safe now. Sweetheart, you'll meet someone who loves you for you, one day." *Could be sooner than you think if Des makes a move on you.*

Carla stared at her mug. "Thanks, not sure I'll be on the lookout for someone to fill Gary's shoes anytime soon."

"Fill his shoes? I hope not. He has been wrong for you from the start, love."

"I wouldn't say that. We've shared some good times together, you know, before his accident. It literally changed everything."

"Are you telling me he wasn't fist happy before the accident occurred then?"

Carla glanced up and shook her head. "No, not at all."

"That's so sad. No sign of any bad temper or anger issues?"

"Nope, nothing. He was always kind and gentle. It's so confusing because I loved him the way he used to be and felt sorry for the person he became in the end. I doubt if you'll understand that, but that's the only way I can explain the situation."

"Maybe something went awry in his brain during the accident. Either way, he should've reached out for counselling rather than take his frustrations out on you with his fists. I don't suppose you've checked what you look like in a mirror yet, have you?"

"I'm too scared to. I caught a quick glimpse in the oven door, it was enough, for now. I'm just sorry I couldn't handle the situation myself. Makes me feel like a failure."

"That's ludicrous. Anyway, let's not get morbid about the past."

She raised her mug, and Carla raised hers. "Here's to the future. Who knows what good things lie around the corner for you?"

They clinked their mugs together and took a sip of coffee.

"Who knows? I'm just grateful for you and the chief showing faith in me. If you guys hadn't come to see me today, I'd be joining the dole queue tomorrow. I'm sorry you had to put up with Gary's foul mood, though. He had no right to attack you like that."

"Not your problem any more, love. You're well shot of him now."

"Dare I ask how the interview went with him?"

"I left it to the chief. She reported back to me before I came home that he was showing little to no remorse for his actions. I reckon he seriously needs help, professional help. You've done the right thing leaving him, love. You know you're welcome to stay here as long as you like. Just muck in, help yourself to food and drink when you want, you hear me?"

Tears filled Carla's eyes. "You're incredible. Most people would have turned their back on me for walking out on the job, but not you. And to welcome me into your home... I'm so grateful to you, and Mark, of course. I'll try not to get in the way."

"You won't, I'll make sure I work you hard over the next few days at least."

"I was expecting you to say something along those lines. How's the investigation going? Or do you have a rule about not talking shop at home?"

"Generally, we try not to discuss things, however, I don't mind talking work when it's only you and me here."

"I'll try to remember that."

"As for the investigation, it's a bit meh, to say the least. This afternoon we received a call about another woman going missing, an estate agent. Can you believe she was abducted on a house viewing?"

"What? No way. Are the cases linked?"

"At the moment, we're not sure. Saying that, I think it would be foolish not to link them. I don't believe in coincidences."

"Bugger. No motive come to light either, I take it?"

"Nope. We've got a couple of women we need to search for."

Carla frowned and twisted her cup on the coaster. "Women abducting women, that's a strange one. I don't think we've come across a case like that before, have we?"

"No, I think you're right. Which is the puzzling part. Something else we need to consider is we're only talking about these women being abducted and not killed. To date, no bodies have shown up, therefore, I'm inclined to believe the abductor's intention is to hold the women. The questions we need answers to are why and where?"

The front door opened, and Mark shouted, "Honey, I'm home."

Sara rolled her eyes. "Honestly, he's not usually that sad."

Carla chuckled and shifted uncomfortably in her chair.

Sara caught the movement. "Hey, he's fine with you staying." *Or are you uncomfortable because a man has entered the house?*

"I'm okay. I'm conscious of being in the way, that's all."

Sara growled. "You do talk a lot of shit at times. Chill, that's an order."

Carla mock-saluted her and smiled. "Yes, boss."

"Hey, you two, how's it going?" Mark walked into the room and kissed Sara on the top of the head. "Good to see you, Carla."

Carla's cheeks flushed under his searching gaze. "Thanks for letting me stay, Mark. Sorry for the horror picture show."

"There's no need for you to apologise. You're safe here."

Sara clutched his hand and kissed the back of it. He was such a special man, her heart swelled with love and pride. She hadn't asked him to offer sympathy and kindness to Carla, yet he'd taken it upon himself to do just that. He truly was one in a million. "We've got lasagne for dinner with chips, is that all right?"

"Double helping of carbs is always something to look forward to."

Sara laughed. "Trust you. Have you had a good day?" She looked him up and down, searching for signs of wee or poo.

"Yep, I escaped all that was flung at me from certain orifices today."

"Good to hear. I'm going to shoot upstairs and get my comfy clothes on. Won't be a tick."

She left the room and heard Mark ask Carla if she wanted another drink.

"No, I'm fine. Let me get you one."

"You will not. You're a guest in our home," Mark insisted.

"I'll pull my weight, Mark, I promise."

"We'll see."

Sara climbed the stairs, peeked into the spare room to make sure Carla had unpacked her possessions, and when satisfied she'd done that, she carried on walking until she reached the master bedroom. Any underlying apprehensions about Carla staying with them dissolved while she was getting changed.

She rejoined her friend and her husband, who by the sound of the laughter coming from the kitchen were getting on like old friends who hadn't seen each other in twenty years. "Glad to see you two getting along so well. I'm going to put the chips in. Dinner should be in half an hour, if that's all right with you, guys?"

"Sounds perfect," Mark replied. "Shall I nip out for a bottle of wine? I forgot to stop off at the off-licence on the way home."

"No, we'll manage. I think there's one in the cupboard." She pointed at the cupboard on the wall behind him. "At the back."

He raised an eyebrow. "A hidden stash, eh?"

"Hardly." Sara chuckled.

Mark placed the white wine in the freezer until they started dinner.

The three of them laughed throughout their meal. Sara was pleased that Carla seemed to be at home. She volunteered to do the washing up while Mark and Sara went through to the lounge.

"Are you sure you're all right about Carla staying?" she whispered, casting a glance over her shoulder.

"You worry too much. It's good to see her smile. I don't mind telling you when I first laid eyes on her I felt physically sick. What type of bastard does that to another human being, and a woman at that?"

"I know, it's soul-destroying. Thankfully, she appears to be in better spirits than when the chief and I went to rescue her."

"Glad you managed to talk her round and got her out of that toxic situation. One thought, he's not likely to show up here and cause trouble, is he?"

"Never say never, but I think he'll have more sense than that after what happened today. The chief would have laid into him. Pointed out his mistakes and made sure he seeks the help he needs from a professional."

"Let's hope he finds what he needs, otherwise I fear for the next woman he takes up with, if Carla's injuries are anything to go by."

Sara sipped her wine. "Agreed. Shh… she's coming." She turned to see Carla carrying her wine glass in one hand and Misty in her other arm. "She's really taken to you."

"Do you mind?" Carla asked.

"Why should I? Misty's main priority is obtaining a bit of fuss."

"She'll get that, for sure. All cleared up. I'm going to love and leave you, if that's okay? I have a few calls to make."

"Of course. Give me a shout if you need anything. Oh, and the towels are in the airing cupboard at the end of the hall."

"Thanks, I managed to grab a couple of my own. I suppose I'll have to pop back to pick up the rest of my belongings in the next few days. I couldn't fit it all in the car."

"We could go together, maybe after work one night, in the near future."

"Cool. I'll have a look on the 'Net for alternative accommodation as well, while I'm up there. Goodnight, both of you, and thank you again for putting up with me."

"No need to thank us. Goodnight, Carla," Mark replied.

"Sleep well, shout if you need anything."

"I will."

*T*he following morning, the sunrise woke Sara at the crack of dawn, making it impossible for her to get back to sleep. Instead, she got up early, before six, and knocked up a pancake mixture for breakfast.

Mark and Carla joined her at around seven-fifteen. She reheated the pancakes in the microwave and placed the stack on the table, ready for everyone to put on their favourite topping. Hers was definitely chocolate spread. Mark declined the offer and left at around seven-thirty; he had a cat to be neutered at eight.

"This is delicious. Do you often have a large breakfast like this?" Carla tucked into her peanut butter pancakes and moaned contentedly.

"Yep." Sara was halfway through her breakfast when her phone rang. "DI Sara Ramsey, how can I help?"

"Sorry to bother you so early, ma'am, it's Jeff at the station. I was wondering if you could maybe stop off and see someone on your way in this morning."

"Concerning what, Jeff?"

"Can't you guess? Sorry, that was uncalled for. I received a call from a concerned father. Apparently, his daughter went missing last night."

"When did he ring up?"

"This morning. He's been up all night, searching for his daughter."

"Okay. Carla and I will stop off on the way in. What's the address?"

"Twenty-nine Tidmarsh Street."

"Carla's nodding, she knows where it is. Text me the details, including the man's name if you would?"

"Doing it now."

Her phone pinged. She read the message. "Got it. Okay, we'll see you later on. Let my team know we'll be delayed, will you?"

"Sure thing. Good luck."

Sara ended the call, gulped down the rest of her coffee and shovelled the last of her pancake in her mouth. Misty wrapped herself around the legs of the chair. "Damn, are you ready to go?"

"Almost, just got to brush my teeth. Hate doing it before I have breakfast."

"Me, too. I'll need to do the same. I'll feed Misty first."

"Leave the washing up, I'll do it when I come down."

"Thanks, that'll be a great help. Come on, tinker, let's find you a tin of tuna." She opened the tin and filled Misty's bowl with a handful of dried food and half the tin. The rest she put in the fridge for later. Then she bolted upstairs to finish off getting ready.

Misty was standing by the back door, asking to be let out when she came down. "Come on, trouble, out you pop." Misty didn't wander too far from the back door. She did her business and then ran back inside. Sara secured the door.

Carla washed up, but Sara insisted she left the plates to drain. They set off in two cars.

Thomas Calder lived in a beautiful manor-type house out in the country, near Wellington. He rushed to open the door to greet them. "Hello, thank you so much for coming." He gestured for them to enter.

Sara produced her ID. "DI Sara Ramsey, and my partner, DS Carla Jameson. How can we help, Mr Calder?"

He stared at Carla's injuries but didn't refer to them. "Come through to the kitchen. Would you like a coffee? I'm on my third cup of the morning."

"No, thanks for the offer, we've not long had breakfast."

He let out a sigh and showed them through to a stunning kitchen at the rear. Ultra-modern glossy white units with black granite worktops. The bi-fold doors which led out to a cottage garden were open, and a gentle breeze filled the room.

A coffee machine gurgled to an abrupt halt on the side. The aroma of freshly ground beans proved to be too tempting to resist. "Umm… is it possible to change my mind on the coffee?" She grinned.

"Yes, of course. What about you, Sergeant?" Mr Calder asked.

Carla sniggered. "Far too enticing to pass up. Thank you. White with one sugar for both of us."

"That's sacrilege. I take mine black, you appreciate the full richness of the flavour, then."

"Go on then, you've persuaded me to try it," Sara replied. "Carla?"

"White for me."

Mr Calder finished making the drinks and carried them on a tray out onto the patio.

"I want to report my daughter missing. It's unusual for her to disappear like this, plus, she was due to have dinner with me last night. She always shows up, or postpones if she can't make it. I'm worried sick about what might have happened to her."

"I'm presuming you've tried calling her?"

"Yes, dozens of times. The first time I tried, about seven last night, the phone rang and then went dead after a few rings. I haven't been able to get through since. I've rung every thirty minutes or so, even during the night."

"When was the last time you contacted her and actually spoke to her?" Sara asked.

Carla withdrew her notebook to take down what was being said.

"Yesterday, just before she left the boutique. She told me she was going home to get changed and couldn't wait to see me for dinner. Does that sound like someone who would go AWOL without telling me?"

"No, you're right, it doesn't, sir. Did she sound okay during the call, not under duress?"

"No, very excited. My daughter and I adore our time together. Please, you have to start searching for her. You know when something is wrong with your child, you just know it. That's how I feel right now. She's missing, and I'm sat here thinking all sorts that I'd rather not be thinking."

"It's best not to go down that route, sir. There could be a simple explanation for her disappearance."

"Like what? I've been out there all night, driving around, looking for her. I went to the boutique first, of course. Her car was still in the car park out back."

"Okay. Do you know if there are any CCTV cameras in the car park?"

"Sadly not. She didn't feel the need for there to be any installed, not with the type of clientele she gets."

"I see. Are there any connecting shops which share the parking facilities?"

"No. None at all. Bugger, this isn't looking good, is it? Her car is still there, and yet she's gone, without a trace." He pushed his cup across the glass table and placed his head in his hands.

"Don't give up on her just yet, Mr Calder. Give us a chance to at least try and find her before you do that."

"I won't give up on her, I can't. She's my baby, but you know when all is not well with a situation. I had the same feeling of uselessness when her mother died."

"I'm sorry to hear that. When did she pass away?"

"Two years ago. Some idiot, I'm not one for swearing otherwise I'd call him a lot worse, was driving under the influence of drugs and rammed into her, sent her car spinning out of control and into a brick wall which collapsed, killing her outright. Tore me and my daughter apart, took us months to recover, and we've been inseparable ever since."

"Does your daughter live with you, sir?"

"No, Ashleigh has her own flat. And yes, I've been there to check to see if she's there, she isn't. Nothing was disturbed at the flat either."

"We'll need her address."

"Flat ten, Thompson House, Wainwright Close. It's in the centre of town, overlooking the river."

Thoughts of finding her dead brother's body in a similar location fleetingly entered Sara's mind. She cast the memory aside. "I have to ask if your daughter is seeing anyone, dating or if she's married even."

"No. She's been let down by men a lot and is now giving them a wide berth."

Sara snuck a quick look in Carla's direction. Her partner's head was down, concentrating on the notes she was taking.

"Understandable. Has Ashleigh mentioned having to deal with any form of trouble in her life, recently? An irate customer, someone close to her work who has been causing her problems, perhaps? Anything of that nature?"

He paused to consider the question, and with a few shakes of his head, he replied, "No, nothing that I can recall. Do you believe someone she knows has taken her? Oh God, I can't even... I don't want to believe this is happening. You hear so many bad things like this on the news, and they never turn out okay, do they? I just want my baby back, and no, I haven't called her that in years, but that's what she is, my baby, and I love her very much. Her mother would be mortified to know that she's missing. Maybe she's up there now, watching over her. I hope so. Please, tell me you're going to find her?"

"All we can do is our very best. I'm due to hold a press conference when we get back to the station."

His expression was one of confusion. "You are? You'd already arranged that without even speaking to me? That's not how I predicted things would work, I must say."

"No, this is unprecedented. I have to tell you that we're dealing with an ongoing investigation. This week we've had three other women reported as being missing in strange circumstances."

He gasped and clasped a hand to his chest. "Are you telling me someone is possibly kidnapping these women to order? Please, don't tell me that. I couldn't bear to think of what may lie ahead of her. I've heard about people being trafficked, taken out of their native countries and sent into a world of slavery. You have to do something. You've got to find her before it's too late and she ends up on a boat, heading for Lord knows where. Oh, no, my head is spinning now. Why did I even consider that could be a possibility?" Sweat broke out on his brow.

Sara covered his hand with hers. "Please, Mr Calder, try and not get yourself worked up. There's no point getting yourself into a state. As I said, we're already dealing with three other cases, therefore, if you like to think of it this way, we're ahead of the game. Meaning that my team and I have a few leads we're chasing up. Putting out an appeal will hopefully bring us more avenues to follow up on."

"Do you know why these women have been abducted? Has anyone seen anything, anyone taking these women?"

"We're at a loss to know why or who is behind the abductions at this stage, but we're doing our very best to try to find out. Is there anything else you can tell us about your daughter that you think will help us?"

"Only that I believe Ashleigh will put up a fight. She's a very spirited girl. One of her exes, well, he was pretty nifty with his hands, shall we say. After she got away from him, she threw herself into keeping fit, joined a gym, started lifting heavy weights. She's far smarter than any woman I know, which is why her disappearance has hit me so hard."

"Okay, that's good to know. I have to ask if you can tell me the name of the boyfriend who abused her."

"I'm not likely to forget it. Luca Martinelli, he's an Italian. His parents run the Italian restaurant in Hereford. Do you know it?"

Sara shook her head and glanced sideways at Carla for affirmation.

"I know of it," Carla admitted.

"Good. Okay, we'll pay Luca a visit. I will have to ask you not to contact the man or his family, just in case."

"Of course I won't. Do you really think he could be behind this?"

"It's another angle we have to delve into, sir. Every piece of information we can gather at this time will be of great importance in solving the case. We have to get back to the station now, the conference is due to take place in twenty minutes."

"Yes, I don't want to hold you up longer than is necessary. Thank you for coming out personally to see me today. I'm hoping, and I'll be praying that you'll bring my daughter back safely to me."

Sara finished her drink and rose from the table. Carla flipped her notebook shut and tucked her chair away.

"We're going to do our utmost for you and the other families concerned with this investigation, sir, you have my word."

"I believe you." He showed them back through the house to the front door where he shook their hands in a firm grip.

*S*ara and Carla drove back to the station in their separate cars. Carla arrived first with Sara not far behind her. Des Williams exited his car and approached her partner. Sara stayed in her vehicle, keenly watching the exchange. Carla appeared embarrassed to see him and began fidgeting on the spot and tucking her hair behind her ears while she spoke. *Hmm... signs of flirtation, good to see.* Sara chuckled. She glanced at the clock on her dash and tutted. *Ugh... I can't hang around here for long.*

She leapt out of her car and approached the couple who stopped chatting when they saw her.

"Umm... I'd better get a wriggle on now," Carla said, eyeing Sara shiftily.

"I'll be around for a few weeks, I reckon. Maybe we could go for a drink after work one evening, Carla? Or maybe the three of us could go?" Des corrected himself.

"Oh no, you two go ahead. My social calendar is mega full at present." Sara sniggered and walked on ahead.

The pair joined her a few seconds later. Sara noted the excess colour in Carla's cheeks surrounding the grotesque bruising that was still showing. Des ran up the stairs ahead of them.

Carla turned to Sara, pointed and shook her head. "Don't start. I can see the cogs turning from here."

Sara hit her chest with her flattened hand. "I don't know what you mean. He's a lovely man, though, don't you think?"

"He's okay, I guess."

"There are some women I know who would be fawning all over him, you know, given his hero status."

"What the hell are you going on about?" Carla shot back, her frown prominent.

"Him, being a hero, or have you forgotten how he helped to rescue you?"

"No, I hadn't. Bloody hell, Sara, he was doing his job, for fuck's sake."

"Was he? All right, if you say so. Changing the subject, I have a conference to attend. You go upstairs, bring the team up to date and start digging into the ex-boyfriend's background for me."

"I know what to do. I'll see you later. Oh, and good luck."

"You, too," Sara muttered.

Carla cast her a wary look over her shoulder and then ascended the stairs.

Sara sought out Jane Donaldson, and together, they entered the conference room where Sara addressed the waiting journalists. She covered the fact that four individual women had been abducted since

Saturday night. She went over the details of all four cases, keeping the specifics sketchy. Then she had to battle through the bombardment of questions. Most of which she didn't have the answers to.

"That's it, folks. All I have for you. We really appreciate you helping us out at such short notice, let's hope it does the trick."

Jane thanked the journalists for attending and dismissed the hungry pack.

"Thanks, Jane, you've worked wonders again."

"You're always welcome. I hope it works out and important information comes your way soon, Sara, for the women's sakes."

"So do I. The longer this investigation goes on, the more worried I'm becoming for their safety. That's between you and me, of course."

"Of course. Mum's the word. Horrible situation. Are none of us safe to walk the streets any more?"

"Hard to tell. Maybe the abductor is targeting particular women. We're doing our best to uncover that side of things. Hopefully, we'll get some calls soon which will help piece more of the puzzle together."

"I'll have my fingers firmly crossed and hope you solve the cases soon. I have every faith in you."

Sara heaved out a breath. "I wish I had as much faith as you do, hon. I have to say I'm struggling with this one."

"You'll come good in the end, you always do."

"Thanks. I have a niggling doubt you could be wrong, though. Time will tell in the end, right?"

"It will. See you soon."

Sara walked upstairs, her thoughts with the women at risk. *I hope the public can help us on this one, I really do. If not...*

8

*L*ibby returned to the lockup the next morning. Today, the fun would begin. She had every intention of returning the previous evening to implement the next stage in her plan, but exhaustion had overwhelmed her, and she fell asleep on the sofa, not waking until the early hours.

Refreshed, she decided she had done the right thing, holding off until this morning. This way, they would have the whole day ahead of them to enjoy what was about to take place. The girls would be horrified when the truth came out. That knowledge alone sent a thrill of mammoth proportions surging through her.

She entered the building quietly, keen to hear the conversations going on between her captives, the women who had made her life hell during her teenage years. *Well, revenge is in sight now. They're going to regret treating me the way they did, when I was down and crying out for others' support and help. I'll see how they deal with the kind of helplessness that seeped into my bones back then.*

The door opened, and she picked up on the hushed voices.

"What do you think is going to happen to us?"

"She seems okay, not violent, well, not really," another voice murmured.

"She was to me," replied another.

"Oh, shit! I'm petrified. Nothing ever good came of someone kidnapping a person, let alone four women at the same time. I wonder what she has planned for us."

Not long to wait now, my pretties.

Libby slammed the door shut behind her. The chattering ceased.

"Who's there? Please, can you help us?"

Libby tapped the length of iron bar in the palm of her hands and then went around the room, dragging the bar across each of the doors. "No one will ever find you. I intend to keep you here for a long time to come, so get used to it."

"Why?" two of the women shouted in unison.

"Because I can, that's why. Do I really need another reason?" Libby laughed, a demonic laugh that escalated the more she thought about what she'd said. It had taken her a while to slot everything into place. To find this hideaway, to locate all of the women. She had it in mind to pick up the other woman later on, but for now, the eagerness for the punishment to start took over. She'd been on tenterhooks all week, waiting for this day to arrive, and now, here it was.

She collected the two chairs in the room and placed them in the centre, a few feet apart, facing each other. *Back to the days of social distancing.* Her mind racing with the plans, she had to take a steadying breath to calm herself. Enthusiastic to begin, she put down the holdall, with the equipment she'd brought with her, in between the two chairs. She opened it, extracted two pieces of rope and set one on the seat of each chair. Then she laid out the other equipment, always keen on organising things to be exact and tidy.

With everything arranged, she walked over to the first cell and peered through the spyhole. Jennifer was sitting on her bed, tucked against the wall, her arms wrapped around her knees. Her head swivelled to look at the door as it opened.

"Are you ready? You're up first." Libby smiled at the terrified woman.

"No, please. Whatever you're intending to do, please don't do it."

"No amount of begging is going to wash with me, Jennifer. Get off the bed or I'll drag you off. Which is it to be?"

Jennifer stayed tucked up in her position for another few seconds until Libby took a step towards her. Jennifer tried her best to back away, but her attempt proved futile.

"Get up! Now!" Libby ordered, her hands balling into fists at her sides.

Jennifer shook her head. "No. I can't move. I'm sorry."

Libby pounced. Her fists connected with Jennifer's head several times until her arms relinquished their hold on her legs. "Get up. I won't tell you again. You're only making matters worse for yourself by refusing to budge. Hey, sweetie, it's no skin off my nose if you want to play dumb. I've waited a long time for this. I have no intention of backing down now."

"Please, why are you doing this to us? Why now, after all these years?"

"If you keep asking dumb questions, it's only going to make your punishment worse. Now shift your backside off that bed and come with me."

"I can't. I'm afraid my legs aren't going to work properly. You've had me cooped up in here for days, far longer than the others. You've given me minimal food in that time. I'm weak, and I don't think my legs will hold me up."

Libby growled and grabbed the woman by her hair. "Only one way to find out." She dragged her to her feet.

Jennifer clutched her hand, pleaded with her to let go, but once Libby's mind was set on something, her determination to see it to its conclusion came to the fore.

Jennifer's legs held her frame enough for Libby to drag her from the room without needing to support her. Once they reached the centre of the corridor, Libby forced Jennifer into the chair and wrapped the rope around her torso, leaving her arms and legs free.

"Don't go anywhere, will you?" Libby goaded her captive.

Jennifer's gaze dropped to the implements lined up on the floor.

She wriggled in her seat, almost toppling the chair in her haste to break free.

Libby slapped her around the face. "Don't fight the inevitable. Accept it, like I was forced to accept it, all those years ago."

"I'm sorry. Please, how many times do I have to say it? I'll do anything to make things up to you."

"Oh, I'm confident about that. The pair of you will be bending over backwards to please me, in time."

"What? What are you talking about?"

"Stop with the inane questions. All will be revealed soon enough." Libby marched across the open concrete floor to the cell opposite Jennifer's. She peered through the peephole and stared at Brittany who was staring back at her. Libby opened the door and entered the room. "Right, are you going to come willingly or are you going to kick up a fuss, risk being hurt, just like Jennifer did?"

"No. I'll do what you want. Please, please, don't hurt me."

"We'll see. Be good and I won't hurt you. If, however, you go against your word, well, there's no telling where it will lead. Get to your feet and come with me."

Brittany did as she was told. Libby pushed the woman ahead of her, retaining a grip on her right arm.

"Sit down."

Brittany fell into the seat, struck dumb by the sight of Jennifer tied to the chair and all the silver instruments lying on the floor between the two chairs. Libby worked quickly to secure Brittany in the same way she had Jennifer. The two women stared at each other, fear and trepidation in equal measures etched into their expressions.

"Okay. Now I have your full attention, ladies, let me tell you what is about to happen. Over the next few days, you guys—are you listening, Amanda and Ashleigh? All of you are going to entertain me. How? I hear you ask. By torturing each other."

Jennifer gasped and shook her head. "No, I refuse to do it."

Brittany's gaze switched from Jennifer to Libby. Her eyes widened, and her head slowly twisted from side to side. "I agree, this is barbaric. I won't have any part in this. You can't force us to do it."

Libby withdrew a ten-inch butcher's knife from a sheath in the back of her jeans. "Oh, but I can, and I will, if I have to. You don't want to know what the consequences are. Even the smallest things in this life have consequences. Do you remember, back in the day, how you used to treat me, ladies?"

Her head swivelled between Jennifer and Brittany.

Jennifer whispered, "I'm… we're sorry. We shouldn't have treated you the way we did. We were young and didn't realise what we were doing back then."

"Old enough to know better, I'd say, and still, it didn't prevent you from getting your kicks out of bullying me. Me, a quiet, unassuming little girl, who kept her nose clean at school and her head down in the classroom because she wanted to gain the qualifications needed to improve her life. Let's face it, I didn't have much of one, you know, being a full-time carer for my disabled mother from the age of eight, after my father walked out on us. But did you care?" Her eyes narrowed, and she ran her finger down the cold edge of the steel. "No, you couldn't have given a shit about what I was going through. The suffering I had to endure. The fact I fell asleep during my meals most nights, exhausted after being at school all day, nipping home at lunchtime to feed and change my mother if she'd had an accident and soiled her knickers, then returning to school for more lessons. Bolting home at the end of the day to tend to my mother's needs again and to prepare the evening meal before bathing her and putting her to bed, all that before I had to do my homework."

"I didn't know any of this at the time," Jennifer murmured inadequately.

"And why is that? I'll answer for you, because it was all about you back in the day. You didn't care what was going on in anyone else's life. Selfish brats, the lot of you. Cruel, evil, selfish bitches."

Brittany's mouth opened, but no words came out.

"Lost for words, that's unlike you, Brittany. In those days, you and Jennifer were the ones ordering the other girls what to do to me, or has that part slipped your mind? Your appalling behaviour destroyed my life." She began walking in a circle around them. "The only thing that prevented me from taking my own life was the fact that my beloved, disabled mother needed me. However, going to school every day, suffering the indignation of being bullied, ridiculing me in front of all the other kids, had a demoralising effect on my existence. You didn't care, as long as you lot came out on top, right? Did either of you stop to consider the devastation you were causing to my life?"

Both women shook their heads. A tear dripped onto Brittany's cheek. Libby leaned in close and removed it with the blade. "Are those tears for me and what you put me through? Or are they for the position you find yourself in today? No, don't bother, I think I can guess it's the latter. Shame on you. However, I'm far from surprised. Selfish to the core, that's what you are now and what you all were during our schooldays."

"I'm not being selfish. I'm genuinely upset by what you've shared with us. None of us knew the extent of your hardship. We presumed you were from a lower-class family, that's why we teased you."

"Teased? Pushing my head into a muddy puddle for thirty seconds at a time, you call that teasing me? It was outright bullying. You got away with it because of who your parents were, and the fact that yes, you were a different class to me. I'll tell you this, though, it didn't make you better than me."

"We regret our actions. It was a grave mistake at the time, but we can't be held responsible for what we did twenty years ago," Brittany said, finally finding her voice.

"Why not? After all, I'm still living with the consequences, up here." Libby prodded her forehead. "You didn't know it at the time, but your actions messed with my head. Your humiliation crippled me emotionally for years."

"How many more times do we have to say it?" Jennifer asked. "We're sorry."

Libby folded one arm over the other and tapped the point of the blade against her cheek. "Here's where the problem lies: how do I know you're sorry? You don't look sorry. You seem scared and in fear for your own lives, but I'm not seeing any proof of remorse."

"You're wrong. We're both remorseful, have been for years in my case," Brittany was quick to add.

"And yet you never got in touch with me to offer any form of apology over the years. Hard to figure out that one, Brittany, if you don't mind me saying. Anyway, let's move on and get the games underway."

"You're sick, you can't do this," Jennifer shouted, her fighting spirit emerging.

"Shut up! Don't say that. Why don't you keep your mouth shut for once in your life, Jen? You can see she means it."

Jennifer glared at Brittany after her outburst as if detesting her for challenging her leadership, at least that's how Libby read the situation.

"Come now, ladies, let's not fall out with each other, not yet. Right, Brittany, you're up first, no arguments, I have decided on your fate for you. Pick an instrument?"

Brittany's gaze drifted down to the tools ominously lying on the floor beside her. She shuddered and let out a staggered breath. "I can't, please don't force me to do this."

Libby shrugged and slashed at Brittany's cheek with the blade, catching them both off guard. "That's your choice. I'll just stand here making crisscross patterns with my knife until you reconsider."

Brittany sobbed. "You can't make us do this. It's barbaric and disgusting."

"No more barbaric than bullying a thirteen-year-old for the rest of her schooldays, just for fun, was it?"

"No. We were wrong. Please, that's all in the past now. You have to forgive us and move on, for all our sakes."

The blade took on a life of its own and slashed Brittany's other cheek, only lightly, but the warning signs were there for both women to realise that Libby's patience had run out. Brittany sobbed until snot ran from her nose and over her lips.

"Let's try this one more time. Choose an implement, Brittany."

Brittany shook her head and closed her eyes. Tears seeped through her lashes and dripped onto her lap. "I can't," she whispered. "I haven't got it in me to be wicked."

Libby roared at the barefaced hypocrisy. "Okay, you've had your chance. You're right, I can't force you, not really. But you'll change your mind come the end." She turned to face Jennifer and held the bloody blade up in the air. "This is down to you now. Choose a weapon, and don't give me any bullshit. In case either of you haven't noticed, my patience is wearing very thin now. Something you should be aware of."

"I'll take the scissors," Jennifer replied promptly.

Libby reached down to retrieve the scissors and placed them in Jennifer's hand. "I've still got 'Billy the Blade' to hand, so no funny business."

"I won't. What do you want me to do now?" Jennifer's voice trembled.

"I don't care, as long as you hurt Brittany in some way." Libby grinned.

Jennifer mouthed an apology to Brittany and reached out to grab a clump of her hair. She sliced through it with the scissors and threw the offcut on the floor.

"You bitch. You were always envious of my hair, weren't you?" Brittany shouted through gritted teeth.

"Not any more." Jennifer laughed.

"Okay, now we're getting into the spirit of things, ladies. Brittany, are you still going to refuse?"

"No way. Give me the ones two from the end on the right."

Libby nodded and picked up the long tweezers, wondering what Brittany was about to do with them.

"Can you move my chair closer and hold her right hand still for me?"

Libby did as she was requested. Shifted Brittany's chair a few inches and then seized Jennifer's right hand.

"No, please, don't let her do this to me," Jennifer cried out, horrified.

"You didn't hesitate when it was your turn," Brittany sneered. "Stop whining."

Libby held tight as the tweezers got closer to Jennifer's hand. "No, don't. Agh…" Jennifer screamed.

Brittany appeared dazed by what she'd done. She stared at the fingernail stuck to the tweezers for a few seconds and then threw them on the floor. "Oh God. Tell me I didn't do that. I'm so sorry."

"You fucking whore. You always were a bloody sadist. Right, that's it. You've asked for this."

Libby held the laughter in. Her plan had worked. She would stand back and let the women do what came naturally to them, tear each other to shreds. She'd let them have their fun for the next few hours and then place them back in their cells and bring the other two out, force them into battle.

Revenge, a perfect blend of pleasure and gratification.

*J*ennifer and Brittany looked a bloody mess, literally, within an hour.

"Have you had enough now?" Libby asked.

The women glared at each other.

"Have you?" Jennifer demanded.

"Yep, you?" Brittany smirked.

"Okay. That was fun. I'll return you to your cells."

"Aren't you going to let us go now?" Jennifer asked.

"Oh no. Not yet. Come on, you're first." Libby loosened the rope and pushed Jennifer into her cell. The woman staggered a little on her way to her bed. Libby suspected her legs had been weakened because of the blood she'd lost.

"How long do you intend to keep us here?"

"As long as it takes for you to realise what you did was wrong. I don't think it's sunk in, not yet."

"It has. You're making a grave mistake. You won't be able to get away with this."

Libby laughed and leaned in close. "Won't I?" She left the room and locked the door. Then, once she'd untied the woman, she saw a tearful but furious Brittany back to her cell. "Go on, admit it, you enjoyed that as much as I did."

"Hardly," she mumbled, flinging herself on top of her bed. "Why are you doing this? We've apologised over and over, but you're not taking any notice of us."

"I am. It's just not yet enough to make up for what you put me through all those years ago. You need to be taught a lesson."

Not wanting to hear the woman whining any longer, she left the cell. After tidying up the tools, she laid them out again and then fetched the other women, one at a time, from their cells. Amanda and Ashleigh tried to put up a fight, especially Ashleigh as Libby secured them to the chairs.

"Sit still, you'll regret it if you don't."

Both women adhered to her warning, their gazes drawn to the blood surrounding them and the implements of torture lying beside them.

Ashleigh shook her head. "I can't do this, Amanda. Can you?"

Tears cascaded down Amanda's hot cheeks. "No, I can't... I'm pregnant!"

Libby almost dropped the knife she was holding. "You're what?"

"I'm pregnant. Around eight weeks. Please, I can't do this, not with my baby to consider."

Libby sighed. "Nice try, bitch." She slashed Amanda around the face with the knife. "Don't try and fool me."

Amanda recoiled into her chair and screamed. "I'm not lying. Look in my bag, I have a scan booked next month. Please, you have to believe me. Do you really want an unborn baby's life on your conscience?"

Libby took stock of what had taken place so far. The boundaries she had pushed, by forcing the other two women to torture each other in a game of 'survival of the fittest'. Huge doubts and the ramifications of her actions bombarded her mind. She paced the floor, sorting through the list of uncertainties and then decided to put the women back in their cells until she'd properly thought about the options open to all of them.

She left the lockup and drove home, more and more perplexed by the situation that had arisen in the past few minutes. She hadn't even considered that one of the women might be pregnant. *So much for my extensive research into their backgrounds et cetera. How the fuck did I screw that one up? All right, so one mishap doesn't necessarily mean this all has to come to a grinding halt. I still have an extra card up my sleeve: Nicole Davis.*

9

$\mathcal{S}$ara was relieved when the phones began to ring. The whole team were at it, talking with potential witnesses. She circulated the room, receiving either a thumbs-up or a depressed shake of the head from her colleagues. She did her best to keep their spirits up by supplying them with copious amounts of coffee throughout the morning and into the early afternoon. Sara even popped out on a sandwich run around one-thirty.

By the time three o'clock arrived, after Sara had sifted through the information gathered, she came to the discouraging conclusion that very little had been obtained. The only redeeming fact was that someone had picked up a possible car leaving the crime scene at the back of Ashleigh Calder's boutique on their dashcam. The man, Greg Marsden, was in the process of downloading the footage for them.

Sara went back to her office, drained from living on her nerves for the majority of the day. Carla joined her with a cup of coffee for both of them.

"How are you holding up?" Sara asked.

"I'm fine. You look as if you're thinking about jacking it all in."

"Really? Maybe the thought had fleetingly crossed my mind, but you know me, I'm not one to give up. Are you really fine? I've been watching you out there, so don't try and pull the wool over my eyes."

"Ha, I wouldn't dream of it. Majority of the time I'm just dandy, and then certain things seem to catch me out and make me take stock. I suppose I've had a few of those today."

"We all get them. It's how we deal with them that can complicate things."

"I know. I'm trying my best to stay on course and not to get side-tracked."

"I have to say, you're doing a fabulous job."

"Thanks. Umm… not sure if I should tell you this or not." Carla's gaze drifted over to the window.

"Sounds worrying, go on." She sensed Carla was going to say something about Des Williams. Sara tried to contain herself. Not let on how pleased she would be to see them pair up.

Carla kept looking out of the window and said, "He rang me."

"Excuse me. Who rang you? No! Not Gary?"

Carla gulped and turned her attention to Sara. "Yes, about ten minutes ago."

"What? The man is a bloody nightmare. What did he say?"

"He was full of regrets."

"Don't tell me you listened to his pitiful apology?" Sara's gaze narrowed, trying to see beneath Carla's unreadable exterior.

"No. Of course not. We're through, over with, and I told him as much."

"Phew, thank goodness for that. Dare I ask what his reaction was?"

"At first he was angry. I almost put the phone down on him."

You should have. I'm sensing the bastard is going to worm his way back into your life, unless someone better comes along, like Des! Behave, woman!

"But you didn't. May I ask why?"

"I needed to hear him squirm, to say the words he's never said before, that he regrets lashing out."

"And did he?" Sara picked up her cup and took a sip of her hot coffee.

"No, not in the slightest. I saw through his call. It's taken me a long time to realise I don't need to deal with anyone else's angst and anxieties. I'm my own person, I have a right to live a happy life, like you."

Sara smiled. "I am happy, although saying that, I doubt if I would be this happy if Mark wasn't around. Hang in there. You never know, a prince charming might be around the corner, waiting to swoop."

"You're so full of shit at times."

"I know, but it makes you smile. I miss your smile. You're such a beautiful woman, Carla—when your face hasn't been used as a punch-bag, that is. No one has to put up with their fella laying a hand on them in that way. You have nothing to feel guilty about with regard to his accident. That's his lookout, not yours. You should be able to live life without fearing if someone will take offence to what you say or even how you look at them. You hear me?"

"Yes, I received the message loud and clear earlier." She sighed, and her gaze dropped. "There's something else I need to tell you."

"There is? What's that?" Sara had a notion what her partner was going to say next.

"I… well, how do I say this?"

"You let the words form in that intelligent brain of yours and it then transfers the message to your lips and the words tumble out. Give it a try, hon."

Carla laughed and shook her head. "You really do talk a lot of crap sometimes."

"I'll claim that, it balances things out, because you know full well, I also talk a lot of sense at times, too."

"I'll give you that. As I was saying before you interrupted me with your nonsense…" Carla paused and ran a finger around the top of her cup. "I won't be home for dinner tonight."

"Oh! Why's that?" Sara asked, feigning surprise.

Carla's eyes formed tiny slits for a few seconds. "Because I have a dinner engagement."

"You have? With whom?"

"You're so full of bullshit, Sara Ramsey. You know who with. In fact, it wouldn't surprise me if you had a hand in the invitation."

Sara flung herself back in her chair and raised her hands. "I haven't got a clue what you're going on about. Who is this date with?"

Carla tutted and sighed. "Please, don't insult my intelligence."

Sara chuckled. "Okay, I won't. Des Williams, right? Or should I say, your hero, Inspector Williams?"

"He'd love that status, I'm sure. Yes, he asked me earlier. Which kind of rocked me a little."

"Why? He's obviously a man with good taste, knows a beautiful woman when one is staring him in the face."

Carla circled her face with her finger. "Hardly, I look like a defeated pit bull after an illegal fight."

"You've got that right. It was *illegal* what Gary did to you, therefore he needs to be punished. Maybe Des will be able to persuade you to do the right thing. Having him as a genuine support might make you reconsider filing charges against Gary."

"Possibly. We'll see. One tiny step at a time for now, right?"

"Indeed. Baby steps. For what it's worth, I think Des would be an excellent catch for you."

"Another string to your bow, eh?"

Sara inclined her head. "What is?"

"Matchmaker."

They both laughed.

"I'll wear that as a badge of honour if he makes you see sense and gets you away from Gary the lout."

"FYI, I am away from him. I'm coming around to your way of thinking, Sara, I promise. It's the guilt factor that's lying heavy on my heart, something I'm doing my best to battle at present."

"Guilt factor? For him being arrested?"

"No, for the accident and what he's had to deal with."

Her partner's words shocked her. "Oh, love, you can't go through life feeling guilty about what happens to others. He's had the best medical advice around to help him get through his ordeal. Let's face it, his injuries weren't really that bad in the end, were they? He still has all his limbs and is able to walk. To some, that would be regarded as a definite bonus."

Carla sighed, stretched her neck out and circled her head. "Possibly. You think he's guilty of laying it on thick, to gain more sympathy from people, including me?"

Sara shrugged. "I'm not really one to cast aspersions, you know that, but all you can do is weigh up the possibilities. How did he treat his mum throughout his rehabilitation? Any different to how he treated or spoke to her normally? That's often a guide."

Carla paused to think. "You're right, I'm such an idiot. He regarded her the same way he always had. No change whatsoever. God, why didn't I see that?"

"You were too close to the truth and you felt sorry for him. Feeling sorry for someone isn't the same as love, Carla, you need to realise that."

"It's beginning to dawn on me now. What the fuck? Why didn't I see him for what he was when we were together? I thought I loved him, but why would anyone love someone who used them as a punching bag?" Fresh tears formed. Carla swiped them away in anger. "That's the last tears I'll be shedding for that fucker. He's not worth it."

Sara clapped. "Good girl. He'll get what he deserves, when the time is right."

"I have some serious thinking to do now that my head has cleared. I never, ever thought I would find myself in such an untenable position. I suppose until something as drastic as this affects you on a daily basis, you just don't know how you're going to react. I can see why so many women defend the men who abuse them, I'm guilty of doing just that. Maybe it should be compulsory that women who have ever been struck by a man get some form of counselling. Perhaps then they'd be able to sit back and take stock like I have. Thank you for sticking by me, I'll be forever in your debt."

Sara's eyes misted up, and she pulled a tissue from the box sitting next to her in-tray. "God, now you've gone and started me off. You'll get through this, love. Don't put pressure on yourself as far as Des is concerned. Take things nice and slowly. It's obvious he cares about you, otherwise he'd have run a mile the second he saw your bruises. Give him a chance to romance you a little. Get to know him for who he is. Yes, he's your senior officer, I wasn't really talking about that. To me, he seems a genuine, trustworthy guy. I have a nose for those types of fellas, so it would seem," she added with a wink.

"Thanks, Sara. If I end up half as happy as you are, I'm going to count that as a major win."

"Why settle for half? Just sit back and enjoy what's ahead of you. You know I'm always here for you if you need to run anything by me, okay?"

Carla smiled. "What would I do without you beside me? I'm so grateful for your friendship and ashamed at the way I acted yesterday. You could have easily ditched me as a friend as well as a colleague. Instead, your resilience showed and taught me a lesson or two. Thank you for opening up your home to me as well. You've gone above and beyond. I'm going to do my very best not to outstay my welcome."

"I know you won't. Promise me one thing, though?"

"Go for it."

"Take your time to get to know Des before you take things any further."

"You mean before I have sex with him? Yes, Mum, I'll take my time in that respect, you have my word."

"Good. Right, let's rejoin the others, see what they've got to offer us. Final word on the subject: have fun tonight, relax and enjoy yourself, don't sit there dwelling on the past, and for God's sake, don't start making comparisons either."

"I won't, I promise."

They left the office and joined the rest of the team. Sara circulated the room. The phones had died down a little, but there was still the odd call coming through.

"Any news on the dashcam footage yet, Craig?"

"Yes, boss. Greg Marsden brought it in about five minutes ago. I'm in the process of loading it onto the computer now. Can you bear with me?"

"Of course. Let me know when you've managed it." Sara brought the board up to date as another call came in.

"Boss, I have the footage lined up now," Craig yelled.

Sara briefly finished off the rest of the notes she was making and raced across the room to see the footage for herself. "Okay, run it."

The image was shaky to begin with but it settled down to show a white Golf leaving the car park at just gone six-ten p.m. "Hmm... interesting. Can you home in and get the number plate, Craig?"

"I'll try." He tweaked the image, and success. "There it is. I'll try and get it clearer."

Sara's heart pounded. "Brilliant. Well done, you." She patted Craig on the shoulder. "At last, we've got something for us to go on. Am I pushing my luck asking you to try and get a closer look at the driver? I appreciate the picture isn't the best."

"Leave it with me, boss."

Sara did just that and made her way across the room to Christine. "Pre-empting what Craig is trying to obtain for us, can you bring up a list for me of all the white Golfs in the Hereford area, Christine?"

"I will. Looking at the social media side of things for all four women, we've linked most of them on Facebook, bar one. Marissa and I are checking out the other accounts now."

"Are they just friends, or do they meet up occasionally?"

"To me, they appear to be just friends. I searched their photos, and there weren't any group pictures anywhere, not that I could spot, anyway."

"That's all right. The fact that you've discovered they're linked could be the key to why they've all been targeted. A loose connection is better than none at all. Don't forget two of them went to the same school. Can you check to see where the other two went?"

"Of course. I'll keep digging, once I've compiled a list of Golf cars for you."

Sara smiled. "Appreciate it."

"I've got it," Craig shouted.

She flew back to his desk, and there, sitting large and proud on the screen, was the registration number of the Golf. "Good man." She wrote the information down and took it back to Christine.

"Your job just got a little easier."

"Here we go. The vehicle is registered to an Elizabeth Johnson of two Harchester Road, Warham. I've not heard of that. I'll bring it up on the map."

Sara watched her punch in the keys swiftly and efficiently.

"Ah, yes, I know where it is now. Small village on the outskirts of the city."

"That's good enough for me. Carla, let's take a ride out there, see what we can find. Stick with it, guys, I sense we're getting close now. Christine, begin a background check on the woman for me. See if there's a connection to the other women."

"Leave it with me. I'll have the information ready for you when you get back."

"You're a star."

Sara and Carla rushed down the stairs and out to the car.

Carol Price was in the car park, just getting into her vehicle. "Hey, slow down, what's the rush?"

"Good news. Possible suspect. We're just going out there now to see for ourselves."

"With backup, I hope," Price warned.

"Umm... no, leave it with us. We're just going to see if the woman is there or not, first."

"Okay, don't go doing anything rash, you hear me?"

"Yes, boss," Sara barked before she slipped behind the steering wheel.

"Sucking eggs comes to mind," Carla mumbled.

They fastened their seatbelts and set off. "Yeah, the thought had crossed my mind to say something sarcastic back to her, but I held firm."

Carla sniggered. "That's because you're a wise woman."

"Debatable at times. Let's hope we're on to something good here."

"Have faith."

Sara nodded and put her foot down. They reached Warham, and the satnav led them to the house they were after. "A small community by the look of things. No Golf here, which is a shame."

"Maybe she's out at work," Carla suggested.

"That's a distinct possibility. Why don't we see what a few of the neighbours have to say?"

"A small community, it's possible they could close ranks, keep schtum and tell Johnson that we were here looking for her."

"You're right. Okay, let's see if we can have a discreet scan around the property without any nosey beaks being alerted. My first impression is that the property looks too small to keep the women here."

"Yeah, I was thinking the same. So where is she keeping them?"

"That's the sixty-four-million-dollar question right there. I'm going to take a walk around the rear, see if there's a facility in the back garden either above or below ground."

"Ooo… get you. All right, I'll take a leisurely stroll up the road, see if I can glean anything from the other houses around here. She could be using one of them, you never know."

"True enough. Look for any signs of a basement in the properties."

They separated, and Sara casually but discreetly went around the back of the cottage, but to her disappointment she was greeted with a tiny lawned garden at the rear. No other possible buildings in sight, and the area was too small for Sara to consider any form of hideaway being underground. *So where is she keeping them? If she has them. Maybe she's kidnapped them and sold them on or something of that nature. I can't rule anything out, not at this stage.*

Sara reluctantly returned to her car where she caught up with Carla who appeared to be as dejected as she was. "Anything?"

"Nope. Nothing. There's a farm up the road. I tried to get a look at the buildings set back from the road, however, from what I could see, they're all being used to store hay. Chock-full of bales, so I think we can count those out."

"That's a shame. The back garden is smaller than mine, no chance of hiding four women there. I'm going to call Christine, see what she's managed to dig up on the woman so far."

"Good idea. It would be a shame to go back to the station if we could be out here, ready to pounce, as it were."

Sara rang the station. "Christine, it's me. What have you got for us, if anything?"

"Not very much at the moment, to tell you the truth, boss. I've researched her background. As far as I can tell, she doesn't have a social media account to her name, so she could be using a pseudonym."

Sara's eyes narrowed, and she stared at the cottage. "It's possible. Does anyone else live at the address?"

"Nothing is coming up in the search. I'm about to do some more digging, go back a few years on the electoral roll."

"Excellent. All right. Well, until we manage to find anything else on her, our hands are well and truly tied. We've drawn a blank here. Carla and I believe the house is far too tiny to house the missing women, and there are no structures in the garden which could be used as suitable hiding places. It's a small community; we're going to hold off questioning the neighbours for the time being, just in case word gets back to her and she gets spooked. For now, she believes she's under our radar, let's keep her thinking along those lines. Christine, do your best, see what you can come up with. We're going to drive around the area, see if anything strikes us as a potential hideaway. Ring me if you find out anything worth following up on."

"I will, right away. Good luck."

"You, too."

Sara started the car and drove around the area. Apart from the farm buildings that Carla had already spotted and disregarded, there was nothing that struck them as being a possible storage facility. In the end, frustration got the better of Sara. She gave up and returned to the station.

"Sorry, guys, nothing out there from what we can see. Any luck with the background checks, Christine?"

"According to the electoral roll, up until June this year, there was a Mildred Johnson residing at that address."

"Interesting, mother perhaps?"

"I'm searching the death records now, but the site is giving me some grief, it keeps crashing on me."

"Stick with it."

Christine nodded and pounded on her keyboard.

"Anything else?" Sara asked, ever hopeful of her team finding a hidden gem that would ramp up the investigation.

Silence greeted her. "Okay, you're going to hate me for this, but I think it's a necessity. We're going to have to set up a stakeout. Any volunteers?"

Craig didn't disappoint. His hand was the first to shoot up in the air.

"Thanks, Craig. Anyone else?"

Will huffed out a breath. "Go on then, if I have to."

Sara winked at him. "Brilliant, thanks, Will. Why don't you guys head off and get something to eat before you start?"

"A chippy sounds a good idea," Craig was quick to suggest.

"If you're subjecting me to one of them then I must insist we go in your car," Will retorted, his expression one of disgust.

"You've got a deal."

The two men left the incident room.

Sara brought the whiteboard up to date with the snippets of information the team had gathered, which wasn't much. "Okay, I'm going to call it. Let's leave things there for this evening. The boys have got the house covered. There's little we can do for now. Go home and we'll start again in the morning. Well done on what we've achieved so far."

Carla followed her into the office. "Really? How come?"

"We've got nothing substantial to go on as yet. For all we know she might have temporarily relocated to where she's keeping the women. We won't know that until the morning. I think we'd be better off going home, getting some rest, in readiness for what lies ahead of us."

"I get that. I just feel we're letting the women down by not being here."

"We're not. That's daft of you to even consider that. We've done our very best throughout the day. The appeal will be aired on the evening and late news. I'll get the calls transferred and tell control to contact me if anything important comes to light."

"I hear you. Sorry to have doubted you."

"Don't be. You're doing a great job, using your initiative. Hey, anyway, I thought you'd be revelling in the chance to finish on time for a change, what with your hot date ahead of you."

Carla tutted and shook her head. "Get lost. Actually, would it be really cheeky of me to ask if I can have a bath when we get home?"

"Of course not. I've got some extravagant bath foam Mark bought me for Christmas you can use, if you like?"

"Thanks, you're the best. Umm… one last thing…"

"Ask away."

"Would you be up to helping me choose an outfit and maybe correcting this?" She pointed at her bruised face.

"Correct it? How? Doh, forget I asked, you mean help you with your makeup, right?"

Carla beamed. "If it's not too much to ask."

"It's not, and I'd be delighted to help out."

*O*nce they were home, Sara checked there was enough hot water for Carla to jump in the bath. Whilst she waited for her partner to have a soak, Sara began preparing the dinner for herself and Mark. She decided on a liver stir-fry, it was one of her husband's favourite meals. She peeled and sliced all the veggies and finished all the preparation in good time. Footsteps thundered overhead. She climbed the stairs to find Carla going through the rail in her wardrobe.

"You need something smart but casual for a first date, it's all downhill after that." Sara chuckled.

"How to keep a man interested, page sixty-five in your handbook, eh?"

They both laughed. Carla withdrew a couple of possible outfits which Sara rejected with a firm shake of her head.

"Something with colour, black is so dreary."

Carla's eyes widened. "You're kidding me? Most of my wardrobe is black."

Sara sighed, pointed, telling her partner to wait a sec, and crossed the hallway to her bedroom. She returned carrying a light-coloured dress decorated in pink, blue and yellow roses. "I was thinking something like this. You can team it up with either a matching coloured jacket or one of your black ones. What do you think?"

"I think it's stunning and can totally see you wearing it, however, not wishing to cause offence, it wouldn't suit me at all."

"You haven't caused offence. Will you do me a favour and try it on? You might surprise yourself."

Carla rolled her eyes. "Is that an order?"

"It could be." Sara sniggered as yet another eye roll came her way.

"If it'll stop you nagging. Umm… isn't there a slight height difference between us?"

"What's five inches between friends? And yes, the dress is a little long on me so it should be the perfect length for you."

Carla took the offered hanger and walked back to her room. Sara paced the floor like an expectant father standing in the birthing suite at the hospital until she appeared again. Shoeless, Carla entered the room and twirled. The dress clung to all the right places and flared out at the bottom. She looked a vision of beauty, if you ignored the prominent discolouration to her face.

"What do you think?" Sara asked.

Carla stared at her then turned to observe her reflection in the full-length mirror. "I was hoping you'd tell me."

"I love it. Des will, too. In fact, I think you'll take his breath away the minute he lays eyes on you. And no, I'm not bullshitting you, I'm deadly serious. I would never set you up for a fall."

"I know you wouldn't, you're too kind-hearted. Crikey, I never thought I'd ever see myself in something as floral as this. I must admit, I'm loving the outfit."

"Correction, you're *rocking* the look. It's incredible on you, suits you down to the ground. Want me to check my wardrobe for a suitable jacket?"

Carla's cheeks flushed. "Would you mind?"

"Not at all." Sara quickly rattled through the hangers and withdrew a pale-blue jacket. "Hmm… it's a possible. Try it on."

Carla hitched the jacket on, but the arms were far too short. "I don't think it's going to work, do you?"

They both chuckled.

Sara proceeded to pass several more jackets, but they all ended up on the rejection pile for being too short.

"Forget it. I'll stick to a black one instead," Carla said.

"Defeatist, no you won't. Here, what about a cardigan instead. I have a pretty blue one and a bubblegum-pink one which should suffice."

"Bingo! And the winner is, the pink one, I think. What about you?"

"It's perfect, in every way. No idea why I didn't think of it in the first place. It's the wrong time of year for you to be wearing a jacket anyway. Now all we have to do is try and disguise those bruises and our work is done."

"It'll take a bloody miracle to cover these beauties."

"Oh, ye of little faith. Leave it to me to work my magic."

"You're too kind, doing all this for me after a hectic day at work."

"Shut up and sit down at the dressing table. One question."

Carla sat and gulped. "Go on."

"Do you trust me?"

"Of course I do, with my life."

"Wow, okay, that's not the answer I was expecting, but it's good to know. Promise me you won't take a peek until I've finished."

"I promise." Carla glanced at her watch. "Time is running out. I'm due to meet him in half an hour."

"Don't fret. It'll only take me five minutes." Sara got to work, digging through her makeup bag to find her old faithfuls, and after applying concealer and foundation she had a great base to work with. She stood back to view the final result. "There, what do you think?"

Carla tentatively swivelled on the stool and jutted her head forward. She let out a low whistle. "Bloody Nora. Is that really me? You've worked wonders."

"I only brought to life the beauty beneath. Embellished the good bone structure you have. So pleased you like the results."

"Hey, I think you've missed your true vocation."

"Get away with you. At college I used to doll up all my friends for their nights out. So plenty of practice, I suppose."

"And yet you never seem to wear much makeup for work."

"There's a time and place for everything. I happen to think being a heavily made-up copper detracts from my authority, if that makes sense?"

"It does." Carla stood and hugged her. "I'm so grateful, for everything. Oh God, the tears are bloody welling up again."

"You dare make a mess of my masterpiece. Go, you should get on the road."

"Thanks, Sara. I truly appreciate you going out of your way for me."

"I haven't. It's what friends do for each other. You look a million dollars. Pass a message on to Des for me."

"What's that?"

"Tell him he's a very lucky man to have you on his arm tonight."

Carla's mouth gaped open. Seconds later, she recovered. "I can't say that."

"All right then, as soon as you leave, I'll give him a call and tell him myself."

"Jesus, you would as well, wouldn't you?"

"Too right I would. Enjoy your date and be yourself. Don't be embarrassed about your bruises, they're well camouflaged, and there's no possibility of that gunk wearing off during the evening either. Hmm… not sure if the lipstick will survive, depends how much kissing you do at the end of the evening."

"Hey, I thought your advice was to take things slowly."

Sara grinned and shrugged. "Do you always take my advice?"

Carla sniggered. "In other words, see how the date pans out and take it from there, right?"

"Yes, see how you click. He seems a decent chap to me, but if there's no sign of flirting during the course of the evening, I'd give him a swerve when he asks for a second date."

"Jumping the gun a little, aren't you?"

"Not at all. Any man would be a fool if he didn't want you on his arm for a second date."

"Let me see how the first date goes first."

They both descended the stairs.

The front door opened, and Mark entered as they neared the bottom. "Wow, stunning, Carla, *absolutely* stunning."

"See, I told you." Sara sidled up to Mark, flung an arm around his waist and kissed him.

"You look stunning as well, wifey dearest."

"Thanks. My jealousy gene was on full alert for a moment there."

Mark kissed her again. "No need. I'm all yours for the rest of our lives."

Carla squeezed past them to get to the front door. "My cue to leave you two lovebirds alone for the evening."

"Have fun," Sara replied with a warm smile.

"He's an extremely lucky man. In fact, I'm a little envious of him," Mark said.

"Gosh, you guys, will you stop it with the compliments? I'm not used to receiving them."

Sara's heart went out to Carla. She held out a hand for her to take. "That's because you've been surrounded by the wrong type of people. Let's hope your luck is about to change, sweetheart."

"Thanks."

Sara watched her friend leave, convinced that DI Des Williams wouldn't let her down this evening.

ere she was, lying in wait, at almost six p.m., nervously surveying the area around her. Her car was parked at the end of a small road—only a few houses here. Nicole Davis should arrive any second, according to the notes she'd made over the past few weeks. The same day, the same time.

At that moment, she caught sight of Nicole's estate car in her rear-view mirror. Nicole pulled up outside the large bungalow and went to the back of her car to unload the two yapping dachshunds. Libby's adrenaline kicked in. She started up her Golf and rolled the car forward until it was sitting behind Nicole's vehicle. She wound the window down to hear what was being said and at the same time preparing herself for action. She ran her fingers over her weapon of choice, sitting on the passenger seat beside her.

"Goodbye, Mrs Synch. See you next Monday. Have a good weekend."

"I will, dear. And the same to you. Thank you so much for taking such good care of my babies."

"Aww… it's always a pleasure to walk Trixie and Barnie, they're little angels. I wish all my clients' dogs were as well-behaved as they are."

"I'll be sure to give them an extra treat on your behalf," the old woman shouted and then closed her front door.

Libby watched Nicole approach her car, carrying an envelope with her payment inside, plus a small tip, she shouldn't wonder. Nicole got closer to her car. Libby quickly exited her vehicle and called out.

"Hi, sorry, can you help me? I think I took a wrong turn somewhere a while back and now I'm lost."

Nicole smiled and nodded. "Of course, if I can. I don't really know this area too well, but I'll give it a try. I know what it's like to get lost, it happens to me a few times every week without fail."

"Thanks. I've got an appointment in Granger Road. I thought it was around here…"

Whack! Nicole fell to the ground with a grunt.

Libby worked swiftly to bundle her body in the boot of her car and then put her foot down on the accelerator and drove across town in the heaving traffic. *The final one, now the real games can begin. Today was just a taster of what they can expect. I'll make sure they enjoy being back together again after all this time.*

A short distance from the lockup, Libby checked her mirror to make sure she wasn't being followed and let out the breath she'd been suppressing for the final part of her journey. Outside the building, she unloaded her package and locked the car. Nicole was lighter than a few of the others, making the task easier than she'd anticipated. She opened the outer door, securing it with a bolt behind her, and then unlocked the door that led to the cells. There was a vacant one at the end, which had been prepared for the new arrival. She lowered the woman's feet onto the floor then dropped her onto the bed. Nicole stirred, her eyelids flickered open, and her hand raised to shield her eyes.

"What the…? Where am I? And what did you do to me?"

"Hello, Nicole. Remember me? Maybe not. Some of the others recognised me, not all of them, though."

Nicole inched herself up on her elbows and took in her surroundings now that her vision had cleared a touch. "No, I don't remember you. Who are you?"

"Libby Johnson." Her lips parted into a grin the second Nicole showed signs of recognition. "Ah, as suspected, you recall my name. Is that all you remember?"

Nicole's head turned to the wall, and she shook it. "No. Oh God, we were so wicked to you. I'm so sorry for the things we said and did back then. We were only children, we didn't know any better, not then."

"And you do now? I'm glad to hear you have regrets. The others haven't shown much in that respect which is a little disheartening, to say the least. I want you to rest this evening. Take in what is about to happen, and I'll deal with you tomorrow, okay?"

Nicole's expression was one of confusion. "Sorry? No, it's not all right. Deal with me? What in the hell do you mean by that?"

Libby laughed. "Why should I spoil the surprise? You'll find out when the time is right. Until then, rest and take it easy. You've been run off your feet all week, walking those dogs of yours."

"How do you know what I do? Have you been following me?"

"Ah, the penny has finally dropped. Some might class it as following, others might regard it as keeping you under observation, but then again, there will be some who might even call it stalking. Either way, you're here now, so make the most of your time off. I have something special planned for you tomorrow."

"In what respect? Why are you doing this? To redress the past? We didn't know what we were doing, not then. We can't be held responsible for what we did as children. Please won't you reconsider?"

Libby shook her head slowly. "No, your actions have blighted my life for years. Caused me numerous sleepless nights and destroyed any confidence I may have had."

"You seem pretty confident to me," Nicole muttered.

"That's because of a recent transformation. The change in me has been significant, both inside and out."

"I can see. It's quite dramatic on the exterior. I can't see what's going on inside, obviously, but I know you don't really want to be doing this. You were such a sweet girl, back in the day."

"I was, and look where that got me."

Nicole held her head low, in shame. "I'm sorry, it was abysmal the way we treated you. I admit it. Why don't we both accept that and move on?"

"That might be satisfactory for you, but not for me. This is all about revenge. Your gang made my life hell, intolerable most days. It's taken me a while to arrange all this, but let's just say you ladies have never been far from my thoughts over the years. I've despised each and every one of you for decades and been plotting this in my dreams for years. Timing is everything, they say. The decision to complete my plan was forced upon me..."

"What are you saying?"

Libby came to her senses. She'd opened up, nearly revealed the truth. She mentally gave herself a good shake to get back on track. "Nothing. There's a bite to eat over there. One bucket for washing, the other to use as a toilet."

"But you can't keep me here, not like this, it's barbaric."

She leaned in and sneered. "And terrorising me as a child wasn't?"

"I can't... remember that much... about it," Nicole stated, tripping over her words.

"Why? Because the results didn't affect you personally? You lot made my existence a living hell. I went to school feeling physically sick most days. Tried my best to avoid you at the gates, but you were always there, waiting for me, to satisfy your daily needs for humiliating someone inferior to yourselves. Not bothering to consider the consequences your actions made to my life. Why me? All I wanted to do was go to school to learn. I had a tough life, every carer does, no matter what age they are, but to be forced into the position of caring for your mother at such a young age and then... to be brutally punished by the likes of your gang, for having the compassion to care for your parent, used to be so demeaning. No matter what I used to say to you guys, you ignored my pleas, just to get your kicks. Well, now it's my turn. The boot is on the other foot, and I have no intention of holding back. I've grown stronger over the last couple of years, physically and mentally, and now I'm ready to cause you as much, if not more, misery than you inflicted on me." She sighed, reflecting on the pitiful way she'd begged them to stop treating her so badly. "Back then, you thought it was good fun to demean people in front of the other kids. Damn, maybe I haven't thought this through properly after all. Maybe I should have created some kind of arena and put you lot centre stage so the others could cheer or jeer you on."

"What are you talking about? What are you intending to do with me?"

"Hush, you'll find out soon. For now, I must insist you rest and conserve your strength for what lies ahead of you."

"What? You can't do this. It's illegal to hold someone captive, against their will."

Libby placed a finger on her cheek and glanced at the ceiling. "Is it? Bugger me, now there's a thing." Her gaze lowered to the puzzled Nicole once more. "Don't be so ridiculous. Do you think I care if I'm breaking the law or not? Punishment and revenge go hand in hand, and that's what I'm craving right now. Enough talking. I'm going to lock you in. There's a spyhole on the door, you'll be able to see what's taking place, and it'll give you an idea of what to expect when it's your turn in the spotlight. Although, your debut will be slightly different. I have something extra special lined up for you."

Nicole gasped and shuddered. "What? Why are you singling me out?"

"You were the one who made a mockery of me in front of the boy I fancied. I was mortified when I saw him laughing at the state I was in, the day you poured a bucket of cow poo over my head after school. My mother…" She stopped, a large lump forming as she remembered the way her mother had broken down and cried in her arms that day. Libby had been forced to set her own feelings of humiliation aside to make sure her mother pulled out of her deep depression before nightfall. Aware that if she didn't succeed, she would have been up all night, seeing to her mother's needs if sleep evaded her. A carer never has a life of their own. Their sole aim is to ensure the person they care for has a quality of life similar to the one they once had, when they were fit and able-bodied.

"Your mother what?" Nicole asked, sympathy resonating in her tone.

"It doesn't matter. Rest." With that, she turned and left the room. She fixed her shoulders back and stood erect, giving herself the strength she needed to proceed. There was no way she'd crumble now, not this far down the line.

She stopped to open one of the cells. Ashleigh Calder moved back on her bed, clearly not willing to take part in the next round.

"Come now, Ashleigh. Time's a wasting."

Ashleigh stayed put.

"Move it! Do I have to come in there and drag you out?"

"No. Please. I don't want to do this. I'm not a bad person, not really."

"I'll be the judge of that. Now shift your arse or I'll shift it for you." Libby took a couple of steps into the room.

Ashleigh propelled herself off the bed, screaming, head down, aiming at Libby's midriff. Libby expected the women to put up a fight now and again, so she was prepared for the onslaught. She waited until the timing was right and leapt out of the way. Ashleigh's head slammed into the wall. She dropped to the floor, out cold. Libby fetched the bucket of water and tipped it over her head. Ashleigh came to, dazed, but Libby got the impression she was ready to put up another fight if it was necessary.

Libby took a hard stance, prepared for a battle of wills. "Come on, give it all you've got. But if I were in your shoes, I'd reconsider my situation pretty damn quickly. I have all the cards at my disposal this time, not you. As well as the odd weapon or two. I could do you a lot of damage, if I wanted to."

Ashleigh's shoulders slumped in defeat, and she murmured, "I just want to go home."

"You might, eventually. For now, we need to share more time together."

"What do you mean, *might*?"

"You'll see. Now get up and come with me."

Ashleigh placed her hand on the wall and pulled herself upright and onto her feet. "Where are we going?"

"Shut up!"

The pair stared at each other once they were out in the hallway.

"Over there." Libby pointed at the part of the wall that had two metal rings hanging from it.

Confused, Ashleigh stared at her. "What are they for?"

"Questions, questions… just do as you're told."

Ashleigh moved closer to the wall. Libby didn't trust her and stayed alert until she'd secured Ashleigh's hands to the two rings. "Good. It's about time you cooperated and stopped playing the big I am."

"Screw you!" Ashleigh kicked out with a leg and caught Libby on the shin.

Libby extracted a metal bar from the waistband of her jeans and hit the woman in the lower back.

"Bitch. I'll get you for that."

"Yeah, maybe you will, one day. But not now, I have the upper hand, and you'd be wise not to forget that—if you want to live, that is."

"Meaning what? Your intention is to kill me, kill us? Is that what all this is about?"

"Hush now. You'll find out when the time presents itself."

"Screw you, bitch."

"That's it, let all your aggression out. You must have been suppressing the real you for years. It must be such a relief to drop the mask and reveal the genuine personality beneath that fake exterior. Mind you, you're not alone. All the others will do the same, eventually. That should make life interesting around here. A real battle of wills… to survive."

"Survive what?"

"All will become clear soon, once I've stoked the fires. Yesterday's entertainment was just a taster of what lies ahead of you all. You've seen nothing yet, as they say." Libby laughed and took a step back, out of reach.

She watched Ashleigh wriggle and do her best to pull her arms out of her bindings, failing every attempt, to her dismay.

Libby crossed the hallway and opened another cell door. This time she beckoned Amanda to join her.

"Please, I can't do this any more. I don't want to hurt other people," Amanda pleaded.

"It didn't stop you when you were at school. You were always an active and eager participant from what I can recall. What's it like to be defenceless and open to attack? Not pleasant, is it?"

"No. I'm sorry for what we did to you. It was unjust and uncalled for. You've taught us a lesson now by keeping us away from our families. Isn't that punishment enough?"

"You think because you let me go home at night that it didn't affect me, is that what you're saying?"

"No, I didn't mean that. You're twisting my words."

"I'll be twisting a lot more by the time I've finished with you."

Tears emerged and dripped onto Amanda's cheeks. "Please, have mercy on us. We were callous fuckers back in the day. I'd like to think that we've changed a bit since then. Can't you move on with your life, you know, forgive and forget?"

"Would you be able to?"

Amanda stared blankly at her and shook her head. "I'm not sure. I think I would, but then, I wasn't in the position you were in, caring for your mother. That must have been so hard on you at that age."

"You truly have no idea. Don't try and talk your way out of this with your phony compassion and kind words."

"It's not phony. I mean what I'm saying. My situation has altered significantly lately, so much so that I'm finding myself looking at things differently now."

"How?"

"I don't want to say. You're going to have to take my word for it."

"I've researched you all thoroughly, and nothing has shown up, not from what I can remember. Anyway, enough of this chitchat, we have work to do. Come with me."

"What work?" Amanda gingerly got to her feet and walked towards the door.

"You'll see."

As soon as Amanda left her cell and saw Ashleigh tied to the rings, she retreated a couple of steps.

Libby latched on to her arm and pulled her forward. "Don't piss me off, you'll be the loser," she hissed.

"No. What are you going to do with her? Oh God, please let this end. I feel sick." Amanda turned to the side and vomited.

Libby managed to leap back, avoiding the disgusting spray.

Libby laughed, goading the woman who seemed crushed by her actions. "It's not what I'm going to do with her that counts."

"I don't understand."

"You always were a dense bitch," Ashleigh yelled. "Think about it. I'm tied up, you're not... you don't have to be frigging Einstein to figure it out, judging by what's gone on around here the last few days. She's going to make *you* do something to *me*."

"Is that true?"

Libby nodded, her head gaining momentum as horror filled Amanda's features.

"No, I can't. I refuse to do it."

"All right. That's entirely up to you. I'll swap you over, and Ashleigh can be the aggressor for this round."

Amanda's hand immediately went to her stomach.

"Feeling sick again, are you?" Libby was quick to ask.

"No... I..."

"Just fucking get this over with, for shit's sake, Amanda," Ashleigh shouted, irate.

"I can't. No, I won't."

Libby shrugged. "Okay, stand back while I release Ashleigh and tie you to the rings instead."

Amanda placed a hand on Libby's. "No, don't. All right, I'll do it. What is it you want me to do?"

"Wait there. Don't try to run, there's no escape, and if you try it and fail, your punishment will be so much worse."

"I won't run. I promise."

"I promise," Ashleigh mimicked sarcastically.

Amanda glowered at the other woman. Libby suppressed a chuckle and rushed to remove a whip from the cupboard in the corner. She lashed the floor with it. Ashleigh's head snapped around to see what the noise was.

"You must be bloody joking," Ashleigh screeched, her eyes protruding in fear.

Libby lashed the floor again, to ensure her captive got the message, loud and clear. "Take this." She ordered Amanda to hold the handle made of bone.

"What am I supposed to do with it?"

"Hold it for now," Libby reiterated. She approached Ashleigh who started bucking like a wild bull.

"Get your frigging hands off me, you twisted fucking bitch."

Libby jabbed her hand in the woman's kidneys. "Hush. Let's have some quiet around here, shall we? It'll all be over in a minute if you remain strong and compliant."

"Compliant my arse. Let me go!"

Libby took her faithful knife from inside her jeans and slashed at Ashleigh's top, not caring a jot if she damaged the woman's flesh in the process. It was about to get the thrashing of its life anyway. Libby glanced over her shoulder at the shocked Amanda who was staring at Ashleigh's exposed skin and shaking her head.

"No, I can't. Don't ask me to do this," Amanda muttered.

"You have to. One more refusal and you swap places," Libby warned.

"Go on, refuse, because I won't hold back," Ashleigh admitted.

Amanda's head rolled, her neck clicked, and she took a step forward. "All right. What do I have to do?"

"Strike her, over and over. Shall we say forty lashes?"

"What the fuck? Don't tell her that," Ashleigh roared.

The thrill searing Libby's veins was palpable. Yes, it was about to get gruesome but, well, whoever said revenge is sweet, obviously knew from experience what they were talking about.

Amanda took a few steps forward and raised the whip.

Libby watched her intently, fully alert, just in case Amanda decided to aim the weapon at her. "Go on, we haven't got all day. Do it!"

Reluctantly, Amanda drew back her arm and swiped the leather against Ashleigh's naked back. The effort was lacklustre at best.

Libby folded her arms and tapped her foot on the concrete floor. "That was a practice run, now put some effort behind it. If not, you know what will happen."

"I'm doing my best. It's heavier than I thought it was going to be."

Libby cocked an eyebrow. "Bullshit! Get on with it. Three, two, one..."

Amanda raised the whip again and grunted, this time putting her full weight behind the strike. Ashleigh arched her back and screamed.

"No more, I can't stand it," Ashleigh cried out.

Libby examined Ashleigh's skin. The welts instantly rose, and her back was red raw. "Again, I love it. Again!"

Amanda paused and glanced at Libby who tilted her head. "I can't," Amanda cried out. She dropped the whip and stepped back.

Libby marched towards her and stuck the knife into Amanda's gut. Shocked, Amanda clutched her stomach, and she dropped to her knees. Blood quickly pooled around her. "My baby. You've killed my baby!"

For one mind-numbing moment, Libby had forgotten their previous conversation. *Shit! The baby. Why did I do it?* "I... I'm sorry, I never meant to hurt you or the baby, you pushed me too hard." She had to think fast. Libby untied Ashleigh from the rings, pushed the wriggling woman back into her cell and closed the door. Then she helped the distraught Amanda to her feet. After taking a swift look around, ensuring all the cells were locked, she marched the doubled-over Amanda out to the car.

"Are you taking me to hospital?"

"I'm not sure."

"You have to, there's a chance they could save the baby, please, you have to try."

Libby's mind was spinning as if caught up in a tornado. If she turned up at the hospital, they'd ask questions she wasn't prepared to answer. *I could dump her outside and drive off, they'd be none the wiser then. Yes, yes, that's what I'll do. There again, I could always finish off the job, kill her and dump her body. Decisions, decisions.*

What an absolute bummer of a dilemma. My carelessness has spoilt my plans.

She stopped at the boot, removed a rug she kept in there for emergencies and placed it on the passenger seat before she lowered Amanda into the car. "Any funny business and you won't make it to the hospital. Have I made myself clear?"

"Perfectly clear. All I want is to get help for myself and my baby. I know you wouldn't really want us to come to any harm. You're one of life's carers."

The kindness in Amanda's voice and her words made Libby pause for a split second. *She's right. What the hell am I doing? This isn't me. Not really. I've spent most of my life caring, seeing to others' needs, and look at me now. But they deserve it. They were in the wrong all those years ago. All I'm doing is giving back. But do two wrongs make a right? Yes, I have to continue with my plan. It's the only way I'm going to be able to deal with...*

11

*S*ara received the call at around eight that evening. "I'm sorry, love, I'm going to have to shoot."

Mark hugged her and kissed the top of her head. "You do what you've got to do, but most of all, take care of yourself. Ring me when you can, to let me know you're all right."

"I'll be fine. Don't worry about me."

She kissed him, hitched on a jacket and flew out of the house and into the car. Mark waved her off from the doorstep. En route, Sara rang the surveillance team. "Craig, it's me. How are things there?"

"No sign of either her or the car, boss."

"Okay, I've had a call from the station. Looks like we've got another victim gone missing. I'm on the way to speak to a witness now. Keep your eyes and ears open. If she doesn't show up, then it's likely our assumption was correct, she's definitely keeping the women elsewhere."

"Is there any doubt about that, boss?"

"Maybe not, but we need to keep our options open. I'll give you a ring later." She ended the call and engaged the siren. It wasn't long before she turned up outside Mrs Synch's house. Sara left the car and rang the bell to the woman's neatly presented home.

The woman opened the door a few inches and stuck her head around it. "Hello, who are you?"

"Hello, Mrs Synch." Sara flashed her warrant card. "I'm DI Sara Ramsey. You called the station a few hours ago."

"Goodness, you took your time getting here."

"Sorry, I only received the message less than twenty minutes ago. I'm here now. Would it be all right if I came in to speak with you?"

"Okay, I'm not dressed, though. I've just had my nightly soak in the bath. The one luxury I allow myself every day." She eased the door open to reveal that she was wearing a lilac dressing gown, her pink pyjamas showing at the collar and the bottom.

"No problem. I don't blame you either."

"Come through to the lounge."

Sara followed her into the second door off the fairly wide hallway, much wider than her new build. Mrs Synch sat in the easy chair close to the bay window and motioned for Sara to take a seat on the sofa.

"Why the delay?" Mrs Synch asked.

Sara blew out her cheeks. "I can't go into details, I can only apologise and assure you that the matter will be dealt with ASAP and that it will never happen again."

"Shoddy, that's what I call it. That woman's life could be in danger, and it's taken someone over two hours to get here to speak to me."

Sara acknowledged the woman's assessment of the situation was spot on. Control had passed the message on to the front desk, and the wrong person had dealt with the issue, or rather, they had set it to one side when a fight had kicked off in the reception area and had involved all the uniformed police on duty at the time. Two families warring and wielding several weapons was bound to take precedence over a phone call.

"It's shameful. Is it any wonder people don't get involved these days, you know, don't bother to call the police?"

"I hear you, and again, I can only apologise. Can I ask you what you saw?"

Mrs Synch sighed a few times and finally relented. "Nicole has been my dog walker for a few years now. I trust her implicitly with

Trixie and Barnie—they're in the kitchen, having dinner, in case you're wondering. Good as gold, they are, a little yappy at times, when they're not eating, that is. Anyway, Nicole had dropped Trixie and Barnie off. I waved her off and took the dogs' leads off, made a fuss of them, gave them a treat and then went into the kitchen. I happened to glance out of the window and that's when I saw a woman approach Nicole. They appeared to have a short conversation and then, I couldn't believe my eyes, this woman hit her. Poor Nicole tumbled to the ground. This woman picked her up and bundled her into another car. Nicole's estate is still sitting out there. Well, I went to the door, shouted out, but the woman got in her car and sped off. I admit, it took me a few minutes to register what had happened to poor Nicole before something sparked in my mind—the newscaster earlier mentioned that women were going missing in the area, and my heart sank. Wait, I thought I recognised you, aren't you the detective who spoke on the TV?"

"That's right. I am. We've had reports of four other women going missing this week. Nicole is the fifth, to our knowledge. I don't suppose you can tell me what car the assailant was driving, can you?"

"Yes, it was a white one. A squat, sporty type, I suppose. Sorry, I'm not too clever when it comes to makes and models. To me a car has one benefit, to be driven, not paraded as some sort of badge as to how wealthy you are."

Sara nodded. "I totally agree with you. Could it have been a Golf, do you think?"

"Hmm... possibly." She shrugged and added, "Who knows? The point is, this woman hit her and kidnapped her before my very eyes. You can call it what you like, but to me, she was kidnapped. I told you lot that when I rang up as well. They assured me someone would be out within half an hour, and here you are, two and a bit hours later." She shook her head in disgust.

"I know, I can only apologise. I don't suppose you caught any of the number plate?"

"No. I was too far away. I'm so worried about her. She's such a sweetheart with the dogs. I judge people by how they treat animals and, to me, she's one in a million. I wouldn't let just anyone care for my dogs."

"I can understand that. Okay, if you've got nothing else for me, I'm going to get an alert actioned on the car. Would it be all right if I send a uniformed officer around tomorrow to take down a statement?"

"Yes, yes, you go. Please, do your very best for Nicole. Do you know what's happened to the other women?"

"Not yet. The investigation is still ongoing."

"Oh my. Whatever has it come to that a woman would want to hurt other women, or do you think a man is behind this? Maybe it's a man disguised as a woman? The way she effortlessly picked up Nicole, I mean, I suppose it could be a man. Or maybe I'm talking out of my backside."

"I'll make a note of that. Can you give us a description of the woman? Height? What she was wearing, perhaps?"

She shook her head. "No, I'm sorry, I'm not good at that sort of thing. I was too shocked to take note really."

"No problem. Thanks so much for contacting us, it truly is appreciated. We'll do our best to bring Nicole home safely." Sara's mobile rang. "Excuse me, I need to take this. I'll be in touch soon." Sara ran out of the house and answered her phone in the front garden, knowing that indoors her reception was touch and go at times. "DI Sara Ramsey."

"Ma'am, we've had reports of a woman having been dumped outside the Accident and Emergency Department. She has a knife wound to the stomach."

"I see, and while that's a tragedy, what does it have to do with me?"

"Sorry, I didn't make myself clear, ma'am," the young man admitted. "The woman gave her name as Amanda Smith. She's down on our records as having been abducted."

"Jesus, all right. I'm on my way over there now. Thanks." Sara bolted back to the car and engaged her siren again. She rang Craig and switched off the siren once she was on the main road into Hereford. "Craig, anything?"

"Nothing here, boss. You sound stressed, everything all right?"

"I'm on my way to the hospital. I've just received a call about a woman with knife wounds. She gave her name as Amanda Smith. Not sure how serious it is, I'll let you know when I get there. She might be able to tell us where she and the other women were being held."

"Shit! Okay, let us know when you can."

"On another note, a witness saw her dog walker being struck and bundled into a white car, possibly a Golf."

"Double shit! What the heck is going on?"

"Pass. Hopefully Amanda will be in a position to give us some indication as to what this is about. I'll get back to you soon. Keep vigilant, in case Johnson shows up there."

"If she does, we'll ring you right away."

"Speak later." She ended the call and slammed her foot down hard on the accelerator, bashing her head on the headrest in the process.

Sara parked in the hospital car park and tore into the A&E department. She flashed her ID at the brunette sitting behind the desk. "DI Ramsey. I've been notified a woman has come in with knife wounds."

"Ah, yes. Wait here, I'll get someone to come and speak with you." She dialled a number and told the person on the other end that Sara was waiting and then hung up. "The doctor will be with you shortly. Do you want to take a seat?"

"I'll grab a coffee from the machine. Thanks." Sara topped up her caffeine levels while she waited. A male doctor, in his forties, came to see her after around ten minutes, although it seemed so much longer.

"Hello there. Sorry to keep you waiting."

"How is she, Doc?"

"Miss Smith has been taken down for emergency surgery to repair the wound."

"Damn, I was hoping to have a word with her. What's her condition?"

"Not possible, I'm afraid. The wound is to her stomach. Sadly, we believe she has lost the child she was carrying, but the knife missed most of her major organs, so that's good news."

"Not for her, losing the baby in such horrendous circumstances. When will I be able to speak to her?"

"It depends on her recovery time. The surgery should be over within an hour."

"Great. I'll hang around here in the hope she'll be able to speak with me tonight."

"If that's what you want. I need to get back now."

"Of course. Thanks for bringing me up to date."

The doctor marched back to triage.

Sara settled into a chair and rang Mark. "Hey, love, just to let you know I probably won't be home for hours yet."

"Poor you. Sorry to hear that, Sara. What's going on? Do you have the suspect in your grasp?"

"I wish. No, there's been a significant development, though. I have to stick with it. I sense we're getting close."

"You do that. Don't worry about me. Misty is sitting on my lap, having a cuddle."

"I'm envious of Misty. No sign of Carla, I take it?"

"Not yet. They're probably having too much fun. You're not going to ring her, are you?"

"No. And if she shows up anytime soon, don't tell her what's going on. She'll more than likely have had a drink or two during the night, she'll be useless at work in that state."

He sniggered. "Yeah, I won't tell her you said that, though."

"No, don't you dare. Hopefully, I'll see you later. Bye, darling."

"Take care. Miss you."

Sara ended the call and then rang the station. She was put through to the night desk sergeant. "Hi, it's DI Ramsey. I need you to put out an alert on a white Golf belonging to an Elizabeth Johnson. I'm at the hospital, sorry, you're going to need to look up the registration number for me."

"Not a problem, ma'am, I can do that. How are things there?"

"The woman, Amanda Smith, who was abducted by Johnson, is currently having emergency surgery. She's lost the baby she was carrying. Not sure how long I'm going to need to be here, but I'll hang around in the hope that she'll be able to tell me something about where she was kept. If she can tell us that then our job is done, sort of."

"Good luck. Let me know if I can assist with anything else. I've actioned the alert. If the car is out there, my guys will find it."

"Let's hope you're right. She still has four women she's holding captive, as far as we know." She ended the call and placed the phone in her pocket. Her eyelids drooped a little, and she shook her head to prevent herself from succumbing to sleep.

$\mathcal{A}$ few hours later, she was woken by someone shaking her shoulder. "What? Oh, gosh, I must have dropped off, sorry about that."

The same doctor who spoke to her earlier smiled down at her. "No problem. Amanda is out of surgery and in recovery. She's awake. I told her you were here, and she's eager to speak to you."

Sara shot out of her seat. "That's fantastic. Can you take me to her?"

"Of course. This way."

They walked the length of the corridor, hopped in the lift and arrived on the third floor.

"You will take it easy with her, won't you?" the doctor asked during their journey.

"I promise. All I need to know is where she was kept. I have four other women in immediate danger."

"I understand. Here we are. I'll be at the nurses' station if you need me." He pointed down the hallway.

Sara nodded and entered the room. Lying in the bed was a dazed-looking brunette. She turned her head to face Sara.

"Hello."

"Hello, Amanda. How are you feeling?"

"Like I've gone ten rounds with a heavyweight boxer, but I'm alive, that's the main thing, right? She stole my baby from me." Tears flowed onto her cheek.

Sara tore a few tissues from the box sitting on the nightstand beside the bed and handed them to the distraught woman. "I'm so sorry for your loss."

"It's going to be hard for me to get through this, knowing that she deliberately killed my baby."

"She knew you were pregnant?" Sara asked, horrified.

"Yes. Do you know who she is?"

"We think so. Elizabeth Johnson, is that correct?"

"That's right."

Sara noted that Amanda's gaze dropped to her hands which were twisting the thermal blanket. "How do you and the other women know this woman?"

Sara watched Amanda suck in several breaths and release them before she answered, "From our schooldays."

"Did something happen back then? Something major?"

"Oh God, why on earth did we do it? I'm so ashamed of the way we treated her. To think it's come to this. To her taking my baby from me."

Sara touched Amanda's arm. "Try to remain calm. What went on when you were at school? If you can tell me that it might give me an insight into what's going on in her mind."

"We bullied her." Another long sigh escaped her lips. "It wasn't just once, it was virtually every day for around three or four years. We were unbelievably nasty to her. All this is about revenge." She shuddered as fresh tears emerged.

"Revenge? Did she say that?"

"Yes, she made me and the others do awful things to each other. I refused to do it. She threatened she would hurt me more if I didn't whip one of the other girls. In the end, she stabbed me and killed my baby. She's sick in the head."

"I'm sorry you and the others had to endure such torment. I have to ask, do you know where the others are?"

"She has them locked up individually in cells. A thin mattress, two buckets, one for peeing in, the other for washing. The water is cold. You have to help them. I don't think what she did to me will stop her from hurting the others."

"We're doing our best to locate them, however, it's not easy. Can you give us anything? Is it a house? A barn? What type of building is it?"

"There were concrete floors. Inside looked like some kind of bunker. I don't know. Things are a little fuzzy." She closed her eyes.

Come on, think. You can do it. If you really try, we can save the others.

"She helped me into the car. I'm trying to visualise what was around us. It was still light so I should be able to tell you, but my mind is playing tricks on me. She hasn't fed us very well. Maybe that has something to do with my brain not functioning properly."

"We can get some food for you. I'm not sure if the anaesthetic will affect your stomach, though. I can ask the doc, if you like."

Amanda waved the suggestion away. "I'll eat later. Let me try and imagine myself back there. Hang on." She closed her eyes once again. "We came out of a metal door. I looked back at the building, and it had a curved roof."

"That's excellent. Anything else? What about the surrounding area? Any other properties around?"

"No. I don't think so."

"Trees? Roads? Was it up a dirt track or situated on a normal road?"

Her eyes remained closed. "Wait, I think it was a dirt track. I remember we hit a few bumps which jarred my stomach and made the blood spurt out more."

"Oh heck, sorry. It's great news that you can remember. How long was the journey, any idea?"

She opened her eyes and shook her head. "I couldn't tell you. When you're in as much pain as I was in, every second feels like it's an hour. I wish I could tell you more, but I can't, I'm sorry. I'm getting tired now. Please do your best to find them. I know we were evil at school but we've all changed so much since then. Libby has also changed. She used to be chubby at school. That's why we mainly bullied her, plus the fact that she cared for her mother."

"Excuse me? Was her mother ill?"

Amanda chewed on her bottom lip. "She was disabled. Before you say it, I know, we should have been more compassionate, but we were *kids*, we didn't know any better in those days. I've had nightmares about the evil things we subjected her to. I have had major regrets for most of them as well."

"So, you're telling me she rounded you and your friends up for what? To torture you all?"

"Yes, ripping fingernails out, whipping bare backs, cutting off Brittany's treasured long hair. You name it. I think that's just the beginning as well. She has a bunch of tools laid out which she intends to use." She paused to catch her breath. "Except she's not the one using the tools, she's forcing the girls to do it to each other."

"Oh dear, it sounds as though she's in desperate need of psychiatric help."

"You're not wrong there. Please, you should be out there trying to find them. I have a feeling that her letting me go… well, it could only mean bad news for the others."

"I get that. Is there anything else you can think of that I should know? Perhaps you noticed a landmark on the road on your journey here, anything for us to go on at all? No matter how insignificant you think it might be."

Amanda contemplated her question for a few moments. "No, I wish there was something, but I can't remember. Maybe I'll be able to tell you more in the morning, once I've had a rest and the anaesthetic has worn off."

"Let's hope so. I'll leave you a card, call me if you do."

"I will. I could do with some rest now. I'm sorry I've been so useless." Her eyelids drooped.

"You haven't. You mustn't think that way. Hopefully, we'll find the building you described and rescue the girls before any serious harm comes to them."

Amanda pointed at her midriff. "What do you call this?"

"Ah, yes, sorry. I'll be in touch soon. Sleep well."

"I'll try. Do your best for them."

"I promise." Sara smiled and left the room. She trotted along the hallway to the nurses' station and gave the nurse on duty at the desk one of her cards. "Can you ring me if there's any change in her condition?"

"I will. Any luck getting any useful information out of her?"

"No, not really. I'll be off. I might pop in tomorrow, if I'm still around. I'll be working through the night by the look of things, on top of working the day shift. Needs must when there are lives at risk. Goodnight."

"Take care, Inspector. I hope you find the person responsible."

"Me, too, before it's too late and someone either ends up here or worse still, gets killed." Sara turned and walked back towards the lift, her mind mulling over different directions she could take now. Once she was outside, she called Craig and Will again. "Any news?"

"Nothing, boss. All quiet, maybe too quiet here. Feels ominous somehow."

"Hmm… okay. Well, I've been at the hospital all this time. I had to wait for Amanda Smith to regain consciousness from the emergency surgery she needed. She told me what she could about the building where the women are being kept. It's not much, but it might help. According to her, there are several rooms inside, she classed them as cells. The women have a bed each with a thin mattress and two buckets, one filled with water for washing and you can guess what the other one is used for."

"I can imagine. Did she give you anything else about the building? Like where it is situated?"

"Patience man, I was coming to that."

"I apologise."

Sara sniggered. "Eager beaver. When I asked her if she'd seen the outside of the structure, she told me she'd only seen the outside tonight. There's something major we need to bear in mind. She was in a lot of pain, I'm not sure how much clout we should put behind what she says."

"Use it as guidance only, is that what you're suggesting?"

"Yes, possibly. She said the roof was curved. Does anything come to mind with either of you two as to what she might mean?"

"A barn of sorts, maybe?" Craig replied after he and Will discussed it.

"I was thinking along the same lines, but the cells made me reconsider. She seemed to think it was out in the country. I asked what the road was like, and she said bumpy in parts."

"Could mean it's a country lane or a dirt track even. I'm trying to think of anything around here, where we are now."

"Yeah, I was trying to do the same and came up blank."

"Did she give you any indication how long the journey to the hospital was?"

"No, I asked. She said, due to the amount of pain she was in, every second seemed like an hour to her."

"Reasonable answer, I suppose. I'll see what I can find on Google Maps, if you like?"

"You do that. I'm going back to the station now to do the same. Ring me if you find anything."

"Aren't you going home, boss?"

"Nope. If you guys are out here, then I'll join you. Keep in touch." Sara hit the End Call button and jumped in her car. She drove back to the station and entered the building. There was a group of uniformed officers larking around in the reception area. Sara stood there listening to them with her arms folded for several minutes until the desk sergeant came through the door behind his reception desk and coughed to gain their attention.

"What are you lot still doing here? You've had your instructions. Don't come back until you've found that Golf, you hear me?" the desk sergeant barked.

The men had the decency to look embarrassed when they turned to see how annoyed Sara was.

"The women in Hereford are out there getting abducted and turning up at the hospital injured, and you lot are in here, wasting time. Tell me how the hell that works," Sara added, emphasising the point.

The men filtered past her and mumbled an apology.

She faced the desk sergeant and raised a hand above her head. "I've had it up to here with people not taking these crimes seriously."

"Sorry, ma'am, you're right. I'm guilty of taking my eye off the ball, it won't happen again. May I ask how the victim is?"

"Make sure it doesn't. She's out of surgery but mourning the loss of her baby. That probably accounts for my foul mood. I shouldn't have taken it out on you. Ignore me. I'll be upstairs if you hear anything regarding the Golf. I'd really like this woman caught tonight, if at all possible. I fear what she's likely to do with the other women if she remains free. She knew Amanda was pregnant and, by all accounts deliberately killed her baby."

"Holy shit! Excuse my language, ma'am. That's just bloody awful."

"Tell me about it. I'll be upstairs."

"Working alone, or are your team coming in?"

"I have two men on surveillance at the suspect's house. We'll see how that works out before I consider calling the rest of my team in."

"If you need a hand, let me know. I should be able to spare a couple of people, if you get stuck."

"Thanks. See you later. I'm in dire need of a coffee right now."

Sara punched her security code into the pad next to the door and headed up the stairs. She noted the time on the clock as she flicked on the light switch. Three o'clock in the morning. *I haven't seen this hour, not fully-clothed anyway, since my early twenties. Those were the days!*

After booting up the computer on her partner's desk, she bought a coffee and settled down. Her first stop was to bring up Google Maps to begin her search. She hadn't been searching long when the phone interrupted her. "Hello, Inspector Ramsey."

"Ma'am, it's Don on the front desk. I think I have something for you."

Her breath hitched in her throat. "Go on, I'm listening."

"Two of my lads have spotted a white Golf. They're following the car now."

Sara sat upright, her attention on full alert at the news. "Sod that. Get them to pull it over. Have they checked if the reg number is the same?"

"I'll get back to them now. Hold the line, ma'am, or shall I call you back?"

"Get on with it. I'll hang on."

He contacted his men via the radio. A siren started up and a male voice said, "I think she's cottoned on that we're following her, sir. We're heading along the A438 from the Swainshill area."

"All right, Connors, keep up with her. Stop that car when you think it's safe to do so."

"Yes, sir."

"Did you hear that, Inspector?" Don asked.

"I did. I'm searching for a specific building where Amanda Smith was being held."

"Can I ask what the building looks like, ma'am? Maybe I know it, or I could ask uniform if they do."

"Okay, I don't have much." She gave him the information, the fingers on her right hand firmly crossed as she spoke.

"Sounds like some form of storage unit to me. Not a barn. Let me do some digging and I'll get back to you soon."

"Cheers, Don. That would be great."

Sara concentrated her Google search in the area where the Golf was spotted and called Craig at the same time. "It's me. We're close, she's been spotted, they're trying to stop her now."

"That's great news, boss. Where was she?"

"Currently she's in the Swainshill area on the A438. Does anything ring a bell around that area?"

Craig issued a few sighs. "Wait, there's a storage facility out that way. Let me try and find the right location. Bear with me."

Sara put the phone on speaker, tapped her pen with one hand and used the mouse to search the area with the other. "Christ, it could be anywhere out there."

"No, I know where it is. Give me a sec... Found it."

"Good man. Where?"

"Kenchester."

Sara zeroed in on the location stated and immediately saw the building. "I've got it. Join me out there, Craig. I'm leaving now."

"On our way. Drive carefully. Sorry, boss, that slipped out."

"I will. Thanks for caring."

Sara shot out of her chair and blazed down the stairs.

Don looked up from behind his post. "Everything all right, ma'am?"

"I need a few men as backup. We believe we've located the unit, at least via Google. We just need to get out there and take a gander for ourselves."

"I can get four cars to accompany you, if you like?"

"It's out at Kenchester. Tell them to head that way. I'll give them the proper location when possible. Don't let your guys lose the suspect, you hear me?"

"They won't, they're my best team. Good luck, ma'am."

"Thanks." Sara tore through the main entrance out to her car. She revved the engine and secured her seatbelt in readiness for her dangerous mission. She had a sudden pang that her partner wasn't with her. *At least Will and Craig will be there with me.*

With very little traffic on the road, she showed up at the unit within fifteen minutes to find Will and Craig already sitting outside. Sara flung her door open and studied the building. "It definitely appears to be what Amanda described. Okay, backup is on the way. Craig, ring the station, tell Don the specific location for me and then we'll see about rescuing these ladies. Last I heard, they were hot on the suspect's tail."

"I'll do that, boss. Let's hope they grab her soon and that she hasn't got anyone else in the car with her."

"Damn, I never thought about that scenario."

Craig walked back to the car to make the call.

"Are we really going in there?" Will asked, a deep frown appearing on his lined face.

"Problem?"

"It's just that, well, what if she's rigged the place?"

"What? With a bomb, is that what you're saying?"

He nodded. Sara knew he was right and mentally kicked herself for not putting something in place before she left the station. She rang Don and asked him to contact the emergency number for the bomb squad to get a team out there.

*S*ara was fed up of standing around, waiting. It had been an hour since she'd put in the call. In that time, she'd received the welcome news that Libby Johnson had been caught. The officers chasing her had forced her into a ditch on a country road. She'd got out of the car brandishing a large knife. One of the officers had been forced to Taser the suspect. She was now back at the station, reflecting upon her actions while sitting behind bars.

The truck arrived, and two men approached to find out what Sara needed. She explained the situation and asked them to hurry.

"We'll be as quick as we can," the man in charge told her.

By the time they had carried out their tests and procedures, and given the all-clear for Sara and her team to enter the property, the sun was rising over the nearby hills. *A sight to behold when the women are set free.* "Come on, let's get in there."

Craig followed Sara through the front door, a set of bolt cutters to hand should they be needed to release the women from their confined spaces.

"Hello, is anybody here?" Sara called in the darkness.

A timid voice responded, "Yes, we're here. Please help us."

"You're safe now. She won't be coming back. We have her locked up. We're trying to find a key to open the doors. Hang in there." Sara shone her torch around the room, and there, hanging on the far wall, was a bunch of keys. "Bingo!"

Craig marched over to collect them. He circulated the room, trying every key in each of the doors he approached. It wasn't long before he had all the cells open and revealed the horrid conditions the women had been forced to live in.

Once they were released, all the girls sobbed and hugged each other.

"We're so grateful. I'm Jennifer Moore, I was the first to be kidnapped."

Sara gave them all a reassuring smile. "You're safe now. How are you all? We should get you checked out at the hospital, are you all okay with that?"

Jennifer glanced down at the fingernails missing on her hands. "I think I'm okay, they've begun healing now. All I want to do is go home and be with my husband."

"We can arrange that, of course. But I must insist you all seek medical advice in the morning, okay?"

"I will. Thank you for not giving up on us. I didn't think we'd ever survive this. Umm... how's Amanda? And the baby?"

"Amanda is safe and well." Sara smiled.

"Oh dear, does that mean her baby didn't make it?"

Sara shook her head. "Unfortunately not."

"How cruel and callous Libby was to her, to all of us."

Sara bit down on her tongue. "We're going to need to take a statement from each of you in the next few days."

All the women nodded. Craig and Will led them out of the building. Sara stood in the middle of the corridor surveying the scene. On the floor, by the two chairs, were several pools of blood. She glanced up to see blood sprayed across the ceiling and spattered across the nearby wall. Horrendous to think what these women had been subjected to, but in her mind, Amanda had come off the worst.

Sara headed up the convoy of cars on their journey back into Hereford. There, the cars drifted off in different directions to ferry the women home to their loved ones. Sara continued back to the station with Craig and Will behind her.

Inside, she told them to go on ahead while she stopped off at the cells. She opened the hatch in the door and peeked inside at Libby who was sitting on the edge of the bed with her head in her hands, saying, "Why? Why? Why?" over and over again.

Sara left her to it, without saying a word. Too many times in the past she'd felt sorry for a killer; she was hoping this time would be different.

Craig handed her a cup of coffee when she entered the incident room. She raised her cup to Will and Craig on a job well done. "Thanks for your input today, guys. Have this and go home."

"Will you be doing the same, boss?" Craig asked.

"No. I have a full-on day ahead of me. I've got a suspect to interview for a start."

"I'll hang around, if it's all right with you," Craig replied with a smile.

Sara was jealous of how fresh-faced he looked at this time of the morning after being on duty almost twenty-four hours. "Thanks, I'd appreciate the company."

"Sod it, now I feel bad for needing my bed," Will grumbled.

"Hey, there's no need. You go. I would be on my way home as well if I didn't have the suspect to interview."

"If you're sure. I'll see you tomorrow then, boss."

"Yep, the dreaded weekend shift is upon us again. Thanks for all your effort today, Will."

"My pleasure. Glad we caught the suspect and found the women."

They watched him leave the incident room.

"Okay, I reckon the café around the corner should be open by now. Fancy nipping out for bacon sarnies? On me, of course."

"Thought you'd never ask. I'll get these, though, boss, I owe you after all the lunches you've bought me lately."

"I won't argue. Thanks, Craig."

*A*fter gobbling her sandwich and ensuring she'd wiped the grease from her chin, Sara went downstairs to interview the suspect. The duty solicitor was on hand and joined them. Sara conducted the interview at seven-thirty that morning, with another officer present at the back of the room.

"Elizabeth Johnson, you are charged with abducting five women in the last week. Holding them captive against their wills. A further charge of attempted murder is also being considered. Plus, the murder of an unborn infant. Is there anything you wish to add?"

"No."

"I need to ask you a few questions to fill in the blanks for us. Are you up to answering them?"

Libby shrugged. "Whatever." She continued to stare at her hands, clenched tight in front of her.

"The main question is why, Libby? Is it all right if I call you that?"

"Yes, it's the name I prefer to use. They deserved it. You have no idea what those bitches put me through when we were at school together. They terrorised me every day for three to four years. Why don't you ask them why they did that to me? I know I wasn't the most popular girl at school but…" She paused and sucked in a breath. Her gaze rose and met Sara's. "They shouldn't have picked on me, they had no right to."

"Did you seek help, you know, from the head?"

"The staff didn't want to know. A total lack of interest in those days as to what went on after school. I despised those girls so much, but at the same time, I admired them for having the strength to be forthright bitches."

"I'm confused. Why admire someone who was bullying you?"

"They weren't restricted. Not like I was."

"Am I right in thinking you cared for your disabled mother from a young age?"

"Yes. I didn't mind at first. But once the girls started picking on me it took its toll in ways I could never imagine. I've lived a life of hell."

"I'm so sorry to hear that. Why didn't you seek help from professionals when you were older? How did things escalate to this, Libby? I sense you're not a bad person, deep down."

"I'm not. They deserved what I did to them. It was nothing in comparison to what they did to me, a teenage girl with no friends to back her up. Who was lost, all alone in the world except for her disabled mother."

"But why now? What's changed after all these years?"

Libby shrugged, and her gaze dropped to her hands once more. "Why not?"

"Come now, something must have triggered it?" Sara sensed it was the loss of her mother, but she needed Libby to confirm the fact.

"Nothing."

"How's your mother these days?" she probed, scratching the surface of the scab.

"Leave her out of it."

"I know the truth, Libby."

"Good, then there's no need for me to tell you, is there?"

"It must have been tragic, losing the only person in the world who knew what was going on in your head."

"She didn't. You're talking shite!"

"Am I? My guess is you've been planning this for a good few years until your mother's passing. That was recent, wasn't it? It must have been intolerable for you to handle, alone."

"It wasn't. I've always handled my mother's care, from the day my father walked out on us because he couldn't cope. It was always me and Mum against the world, until her death."

"And her death triggered your revenge tactics, right?"

Libby threw herself back in the chair. "Yes, yes. For the first time in my life, I experienced freedom, a freedom that I found liberating. It gave me the courage to right the wrongs people had done."

"How far would you have gone if we hadn't caught you?"

She sat forward again and smiled. "All the way, except they would have ended up killing each other. I was building up to that."

"What happened to prevent your plans being successful?"

It was a long time before Libby responded. With tears in her eyes, she whispered, "I killed the baby."

"Why did you do it?"

Libby gulped, and the tears fell onto the table. "At first, I was sorry I'd hurt her and the baby but then, oh, I don't know, maybe I thought it would be better off."

"What? Because of who the mother was?"

Libby nodded, and Sara shook her head, dismayed to hear her excuse. *What a mixed-up young lady you must be. All because of the way society has treated you, or these women in particular.*

Sara's heart ached. She decided to end the interview there.

She asked the uniformed officer present to return Libby to her cell. Libby mumbled an apology before she left the room.

Sara showed the solicitor to the main entrance and slowly ascended the stairs. She entered the incident room to find Carla and the rest of the team, bar Will, all waiting to hear what the suspect had to say. Sara filled them in then flopped into a nearby chair, exhausted.

"Hey, why don't you go home and grab a few hours' rest?" Carla dragged her chair beside Sara.

"I'll be fine. Let me tackle the post and fill the chief in then, and only then, I'll consider going home. Enough about work, how was your date last night?"

Carla's cheeks flared up. "Our dinner was fabulous. I think I'm going to enjoy getting to know Inspector Williams."

Sara leaned forward and whispered, "Is he a good kisser?"

Her question prompted Carla to slap her arm. "That would be telling."

"Bugger off. Look at the bloody smile on your face. I'm so happy for you, love. Genuinely happy."

"Baby steps, remember?"

"I know. Right, back to work. Can you organise the statements for me? Also, can you ring each of the women? Leave it an hour or so, let them rest some more, find out how they're bearing up and see if any of them need any medical treatment. They were determined to get home last night, and who could blame them?"

"Leave it with me."

EPILOGUE

$\mathcal{O}$ ver the next few days, Sara and Carla visited all the women to ensure they were coping with what they'd been subjected to. They all had their own tale to tell about their abduction and they were all devastated by the way Amanda's life had been traumatised.

Upon reflection, they all insisted they deserved what Libby had done to them. Each of them had regrets for the callous way they'd treated Libby during their schooldays.

Their attitudes surprised Sara. She had expected at least some of them to have been angry and vengeful, even. But the opposite was true.

The court case had been set for four months' time. Libby, whilst on remand, had gone into her shell, and the staff were very concerned about her mental state. So much so that they'd put her on suicide watch. Sara was mystified by Libby's behaviour.

She reflected on the case over dinner one night with Carla. Mark was working late, carrying out an emergency operation on a terrier.

"You think this all came about when her mother died, is that it?" Carla said, tucking into her salad.

"It has to be the trigger. I had a word with the doctor. Her mother was given six months to live. Long enough for Libby to make all the necessary preparations."

"Like find the lockup?"

Sara nodded. "Something tells me when we look into who owns that place, a relative's name is going to crop up. Otherwise, how else would she get her hands on it?"

"Yeah, maybe. She must have a truly devious mind to have followed the women for months, studying each of their routines."

Sara picked up a stick of celery and took a chunk out of it. "Hey, enough about that, tell me about this flat you've seen. Is it one bed or two?"

"One. It's in the centre of town, close to all the amenities. I'm going to pick up the keys on Wednesday. I can't thank you enough for letting me stay here, Sara. Not sure what I would have done if you hadn't stepped in to save the day."

"You would have coped. Are we going to mention the elephant in the room?"

"Which one? Gary or Des?" Carla asked warily.

"Both. Let's start with the bad first. How are you doing getting over him?"

"You'll be pleased to know I'm free of him now, well and truly over him."

"Fantastic. Let me think what the contributing factor can be for that." She placed a finger and thumb around her chin and pensively looked at the wall.

Carla shook her head and laughed. "You can be such a nightmare at times. Yes, it's all Des's fault."

"I'm only teasing. I don't have to tell you how happy I am for you. What about the distance?"

"It's not that far. He's still working with the other team for now, but when he has to return to Worcester, well, it's less than an hour by train, not that far really, is it?"

"Worth the trip, I'd say." Sara winked. She raised her glass of wine and chinked it against Carla's. "To a bright future for us all."

"To a bright future." Carla sipped her drink and glanced over the top of her glass, a mischievous twinkle developing in her eye.

THE END

*T*hank you for reading this gripping thriller in the DI Sara Ramsey series. The team will be back in a few months with more heart stopping moments. In the meantime, maybe you'd like to try another of my edge-of-your-seat thriller series. Grab the first book in the bestselling Justice series here, CRUEL JUSTICE

The debut book in the spin-off series can also be found here. **Gone in Seconds**

*O*r perhaps you'd prefer to try one of my other police procedural series, the DI Kayli Bright series here, **The Missing Children.**

*O*r maybe you'll enjoy the DI Sally Parker series set in Norfolk, UK. **WRONG PLACE.**

*A*lso, why not try my super successful, police procedural series set in Hereford. Find the first book in the DI Sara Ramsey series here. **No Right To Kill.**

The first book in the gritty HERO series can be found here. **TORN APART**

Thank you for your incredible support.

If you've enjoyed this story please consider leaving a review or possibly telling a friend.

Mel XX

KEEP IN TOUCH WITH M A COMLEY

Pick up a FREE novella by signing up to my newsletter today.
https://BookHip.com/WBRTGW

BookBub
www.bookbub.com/authors/m-a-comley

Blog
http://melcomley.blogspot.com

Join my special Facebook group to take part in monthly giveaways.

Readers' Group

Made in the USA
Coppell, TX
05 August 2021